HAUNTED

THE KNIGHT IN THE SHADOWS

ALSO BY CHRIS EBOCH:

HAUNTED:
THE GHOST ON THE STAIRS
THE RIVERBOAT PHANTOM

HAUNTED
THE KNIGHT IN THE SHADOWS

CHRIS EBOCH

ALADDIN
NEW YORK LONDON TORONTO SYDNEY

This book is a work of fiction. Any references to historical events, real people, or real locales are used fictitiously. Other names, characters, places, and incidents are the product of the author's imagination, and any resemblance to actual events or locales or persons, living or dead, is entirely coincidental.

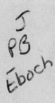ALADDIN

An imprint of Simon & Schuster Children's Publishing Division

1230 Avenue of the Americas, New York, NY 10020

First Aladdin paperback edition October 2009

Text copyright © 2009 by Chris Eboch

All rights reserved, including the right of reproduction in whole or in part in any form.

ALADDIN is a trademark of Simon & Schuster, Inc., and related logo is a registered trademark of Simon & Schuster, Inc.

For information about special discounts for bulk purchases, please contact Simon & Schuster Special Sales at 1-866-506-1949 or business@simonandschuster.com.

The Simon & Schuster Speakers Bureau can bring authors to your live event. For more information or to book an event contact the Simon & Schuster Speakers Bureau at 1-866-248-3049 or visit our website at www.simonspeakers.com.

Designed by Lisa Vega

The text of this book was set in Minister Std.

Manufactured in the United States of America

10 9 8 7 6 5 4 3 2 1

Library of Congress Control Number 2009922366

ISBN 978-1-4169-7550-2

ISBN 978-1-4169-9687-3 (eBook)

For the Society of Children's Book Writers and
Illustrators, and especially the Regional Advisors,
for years of support and friendship

ACKNOWLEDGMENTS

Thanks to Kim Klimek for her help with the Middle French language. The museums in this book are based on The Metropolitan Museum of Art and The Cloisters in New York City, but are not meant to exactly portray those wonderful institutions.

CHAPTER
1

Tania leaned toward the mirror and bared her fangs. "What do you think?"

"Great," I said. "You've never looked better."

She turned and stuck out her tongue at me. It looked really funny with the fake vampire teeth on either side.

"You look gorgeous, darling," said Lionel, the make-up artist. "It just needs one more thing." He picked up a tube. He squeezed a dribble of red along the side of her chin, as if the fangs were dripping blood.

Tania checked the mirror again. "Thanks, Lionel. This is great!"

I had to admit, going as a vampire was a good choice for Tania. She's so skinny and pale anyway. Lionel only had to add some shadows under her eyes, paint her lips red, and attach the fangs. The black cloak with a high collar did the rest.

I looked at myself in the mirror and fiddled with my

lab coat. It wasn't much, as costumes go. The lab coat, a beaker to carry, and I was a scientist. It was comfortable, though, and I didn't have to wear any gunk on my face. The scientist thing was kind of a dig at my stepfather, Bruce. My real father is a scientist, and Bruce . . . well, let's just say he isn't.

"You guys ready to party?"

I turned at the sound of Maggie's voice. "Wow!" The word was out before I realized I was going to speak. I felt myself blushing.

Maggie, the production assistant, laughed. "Thanks." She was dressed like a gypsy. Her dark hair curled around her shoulders. She was wearing a loose blouse and full skirts, and gold bangles up her arms.

"You look gorgeous," Tania said.

Maggie grinned at her. "And you look . . . dangerous."

"Really?" Tania turned to the mirror and smiled at her reflection.

"And Jon . . ." Maggie studied me while my heart pounded.

"Jon," Lionel said, "is not quite finished. Here you go." He handed me a glass beaker filled with bubbling, yellowish-green goop. Smoke rose from it.

"Cool," I said. After all, if I was going to go to this costume party as a scientist, I ought to go as a mad one.

Maggie laughed. "Excellent! And Lionel . . ." Maggie shook her head. "You look disgusting."

He grinned through the fake scar that twisted his face. "Aw, Maggie, my love, that's the nicest thing you've ever said to me." He also had a bullet hole in his forehead, and a couple of gross knife wounds in his arm, with the flesh hanging open. It was great.

"Your mom and Bruce are already upstairs," Maggie said to us. "The party starts in a few minutes. I thought we might go by the Arms and Armor department first."

"Sure, great." I'd follow Maggie anywhere.

"Would this little detour have anything to do with the rumors I've been hearing?" Lionel asked.

"It's amazing how well your brain works with that hole in your head," Maggie said. "Yes, I thought the kids might like to see the site of the, um, mysterious occurrences."

"What's going on?" Tania asked, way too bouncy for a vampire. "You said something about that before, about something strange at this museum."

"The museum has a new acquisition," Maggie said. "A Renaissance French sword they got a few months ago. Since then, they've been having some trouble getting it to stay in place."

"You mean the sword moves on its own?" I asked.

Maggie shrugged. "No one's actually seen it move.

3

At least, no one reliable. But the sword keeps falling out of its holder. They find it in the bottom of the case, or leaning against the wall. Once, several tourists were in the next room and said they heard the *clang*. One man said he saw the sword vibrating before it fell. But he may have just been trying to get attention."

"Yeah, we've seen enough people like that," Lionel said.

"Anyway," Maggie said, "it's strange because there are other swords in that room—two in that case, in fact. None of them have had any problems. If it was, I don't know, miniature earthquakes or something, you'd think it would affect all the swords."

Lionel shrugged. "It sounds like they just didn't do a very good job with the holder for that one."

Maggie grinned. "That's the obvious answer. At first, they kept adjusting the hanger. Then they put in a whole new one. Finally they switched that sword with another one. But it keeps happening, always to the same sword, wherever they put it. Oh, and apparently it gets really cold in that room."

"Weird," I said.

"Let's go look!" Tania's eyes were shining, and I knew this was more than just casual curiosity to her.

We headed out of the storeroom we'd been using for the costuming, and up in the elevator. We'd just arrived that day, and hadn't seen much of the museum. So far, we'd been busy getting ready for the big *Haunted* costume party. My stepfather, Bruce, was the show's host, and my mom was a producer. They'd been worried about ratings, and had come up with this party as a way to get some publicity. I was just glad to get a free trip to New York City.

We went through a couple of rooms full of sculptures to the main room of the Arms and Armor section. It looked like these four mounted knights were coming right at you—but the armor, for men and horses, was just floating, with no bodies inside.

Glass cases around the room held armor and weapons. Colorful European flags hung from the walls. Side rooms had signs that said JAPANESE SWORDS; ISLAMIC ARMS AND ARMOR; AMERICAN ARMS; EUROPEAN FIREARMS; and more.

"It's over here," Maggie said, going through the arch labeled EUROPEAN EDGED WEAPONS. This room was only a few paces across, and dimly lit.

"Brrr." I shivered, but stepped forward to get a closer look at the swords hanging on the wall behind glass.

Tania grabbed my arm and held me back. When I glanced at her, she made this face and kind of motioned with her eyes. She nudged me sideways, and I got it. There was something in the room that I couldn't see, and she didn't want me to walk through it—or him.

5

CHAPTER 2

Tania grinned. She loves this kind of thing. I wanted to ask what she saw, but I couldn't with Maggie and Lionel there.

"That one," Maggie said.

"It doesn't look like anything special," Lionel said. The sword was about three feet long, with a narrow, shiny steel blade, and a leather-covered hilt. It wasn't fancy, like some of the other swords, but it looked clean and sharp.

I glanced at Tania. She wasn't looking at the sword, but was smiling toward the corner of the room. She looked even more like a vampire in the wavery reflection in the glass case.

"It's not doing anything now," Lionel said. He tapped on the glass, as if he could wake up the sword.

I felt a chill, like a blast from an air conditioner. I stepped back just as Maggie and Lionel did the same. We looked at one another and exchanged sheepish grins.

"They certainly seem to have a problem with their temperature control," Maggie said. "Anyway, we'd better get to the party. We don't want to keep everyone waiting."

I hung back with Tania as Maggie and Lionel went out. "So what did you see?"

She smiled up at me and lisped around her fangs. "It's a ghost! He was kind of keeping away from us, watching. But then when Lionel tapped on the glass, the ghost moved over there fast. He stood between Lionel and the sword—right in the middle of the glass!"

I guess I wasn't surprised that she'd found a ghost. In a city the size of New York, it would be more surprising if she *didn't* find one. It was surprising that she didn't see them all over the place. We hadn't figured it all out, but apparently only a few people became ghosts.

Tania's goal in life was to help those ghosts deal with whatever was keeping them here, so they could move on. My goal was to stay out of trouble while I helped her. So far, she'd been a lot more successful than I had.

Maggie looked back and waited for us to catch up. I could hear voices and laughter ahead. "The party's in the Sculpture Court," Maggie said.

We stepped into a huge room with a high glass ceiling. Sculptures lined the walls, but the center of the room was open. A few dozen people stood around, most with glasses or little plates of food in their hands. Everyone was in costume, some simple and some fancy. One woman had a heavy velvet gown that she might have stolen from a movie about Queen Elizabeth. One guy was actually wearing chain mail. I wondered how much it weighed. Someone else was in a big wolf suit.

Lionel rubbed his hands together. "Oh, I just love New York!"

Tania tugged on my sleeve. "We need to get back there and talk to the ghost!"

"Uh-huh. There's Mom." She was dressed like a fairy, in this pink dress, with a sparkly tiara and a wand. Bruce was even worse. I think he was trying to dress up like Shakespeare or something, with puffy shorts and a big lace collar.

"You'd think that since they're supposed to be ghost trackers, they'd dress like ghosts," I muttered as they headed toward us.

Maggie overheard. "They thought it would look like they weren't taking ghosts seriously. Bruce wanted to go as a psychic investigator, with some of his gadgets. But your mom convinced him that wasn't really a costume."

"Whatever." I leaned down for Mom's kiss, glancing around to make sure nobody else was watching. Bruce slapped me on the back. They gushed over Tania's costume.

8

"But, Jon," Mom said, "I still wish you would at least have tried on—"

"Nope. Nuh-uh. Don't even say it."

Maggie raised an eyebrow while Bruce chuckled. Mom just sighed. She's always loved to play dress-up. She has pictures of me in a pumpkin costume when I was a baby. Her taste hasn't gotten much better.

More people were coming in. The noise level rose. "Let's get some food," I said. I hoped they had something real and not just weird little things you couldn't identify.

I headed for the snack tables. Mom and Bruce went off to chat with some people. Maggie and Lionel stopped to talk to one of the cameramen.

Tania grabbed my arm. "Quick, we can get back to the ghost."

"But I'm hungry!"

She rolled her eyes. "So you'll still be hungry when we're done. Come on."

I grumbled but followed her. We slipped through the crowd and back toward the entrance we'd come in. I saw a guard in the next room, but he didn't stop us. The museum was closed, except for the party, but I guess they didn't mind if guests looked around.

Tania led the way back to the Arms and Armor room. I glanced back and saw the guard following us, but he kept his distance.

"There he is," Tania whispered, ducking into the little side room. She smiled at the empty space. "Hello! My name is Tania. What's yours?"

She frowned and glanced at me. "He's whispering something, but I can't understand. And he keeps crossing himself."

"Uh, Tania, you know you look like you're ready to dig your fangs into someone." I gestured toward her, and realized I was holding the bubbling beaker in that hand. I guess I looked a little strange too.

Tania's hand flew to her mouth. "Oh! But this isn't anything real." She started tugging at her fangs, but Lionel had used some kind of makeup glue that didn't come off easily. "Darn it! But look, these are just fake." She leaned forward, pulling her lips back to show the fangs.

A blast of cold exploded in the room. I flew backward and slammed into the wall.

CHAPTER

My head rang; my vision blurred and danced with spots. I slumped against the wall, my legs trembling like jelly.

The cold washed over me in waves. I felt sick with fear.

I pushed myself along the wall, grabbing Tania as I headed for the doorway. We stumbled out of the little room with the cold pushing us like a hand to the back.

"What are you kids doing back there?"

I tried to focus on the gruff voice. The museum guard stood a few paces away.

I cleared my throat. "Just looking at stuff."

"What was that noise?" He took a step closer, frowning in suspicion.

"Noise?" Had the ghost made a sound? It had all happened so fast.

"That bang—like you were pounding on the case or something."

"Oh. I tripped and hit the wall. That's all." I realized I was still holding the beaker, squeezing it like I could break it with my bare hand. My lab coat was splattered, but at least I hadn't dropped the beaker and spilled gunk all over the floor. I told my fingers to relax. After a minute, they obeyed.

Tania was still trembling at my side. Her face looked kind of blue, but I guess with the makeup the guard didn't notice anything strange. I took a couple more steps away from the ghost room, dragging her with me.

"You'd better get back to the party," the guard said. "Save your tour for some other time."

I nodded and we went past him. Couldn't he feel the cold? Or was it all inside Tania and me now?

By the time we got back to the crowd in the sculpture courtyard, I was feeling halfway normal again. The queasy, scared feeling was fading, along with the chill. Tania looked like an eleven-year-old vampire who'd missed her nightly dose of blood.

"You okay?" I asked.

She nodded. "We scared him."

"*We* scared *him*?"

"Didn't you feel it? All that fear?"

Aha. So that feeling of fear had come from the ghost, along with the cold. And I'd thought it was just me. I didn't feel like such a coward after all. "Well, sis, you're enough to scare anyone."

She just sighed. "I forgot about our costumes. That was stupid. He didn't get it."

I thought about it. "If he has something to do with that sword, he's probably from the same time. What was it, sixteenth century?" I grinned down at her. "He probably thought you were a real vampire."

She wrinkled her nose. "And who knows what he thought you were. Did they have mad scientists back then?"

I shrugged. And then I winced. "Look out. There's a real monster coming."

Madame Natasha swooped toward us. She had on lots of makeup, a long, flowing dress, and colorful scarves. I couldn't tell if she was supposed to be in costume or not.

The fake psychic stopped in front of us with an evil smile. Tania and I just stared at her. There was no point in pretending that we were friends.

"There you are, my dear." She spoke to Tania, ignoring me. "I'm looking forward to working with you again soon."

Tania made a face.

Madame Natasha's tone hardened. "You don't have to like me, but you *will* work with me. Remember our bargain. You tell me what you see and what the ghosts do and say."

"And you'll take credit for it," Tania said.

"It's the way you wanted it," Madame Natasha hissed. "You don't want anyone to know about your gift."

"Right. But that doesn't mean I need or want your help." Tania crossed her arms and glared at the psychic, who glared back.

"If you want me to keep your secret, you have to do something for me in return."

Tania's gaze wavered. "I know."

I shoved in between them. "Look, next time we're on a shoot, you can try your blackmail. This is just a party. Shouldn't you be trying to impress people?"

Madame Natasha turned her glare on me, gave a sniff, then stalked away.

I realized I was shaking. She was worse than the ghost. Tania didn't want anyone to know about her gift—if you could call it that. She didn't want people laughing at her, thinking she was lying. She didn't want people trying to use her.

But that's just what Madame Natasha was trying to do. The fake psychic had figured out that Tania could see ghosts. Now Tania was supposed to feed her information so Madame N could take the credit and look good on TV.

I don't think I'd ever liked anyone less.

After that, the party was pretty boring, since the guests were all grown-ups. At least we'd gotten to know some of the *Haunted* crew during the two shoots we'd been on. Most of them were pretty nice. Except for Madame Natasha, who wasn't really crew—she was a "guest star." And Mean Mick. I wasn't sure what his job was, except to annoy people. He hated kids in general, and me in particular.

We talked with Lionel, Maggie, and one of the cameramen for a while. Bruce and Mom were busy schmoozing. They were trying to get advertisers interested in the show, and convince newspapers and magazines to write about it.

Tania didn't say a whole lot. I hated to think what was going on inside her head. I figured I would find out all too soon.

Sure enough, close to midnight, she turned to me with a look I knew well. "It's going to take a while for everyone to get out of their costumes and pack up."

"Uh-huh."

"We have to get back to the ghost without our costumes."

"Oh, right. Only thing is, there are guards in the museum."

"So we have to be sneaky."

"And Mom and Bruce and everyone will be waiting for us."

"So we have to be quick. But I want to go back and talk to that ghost. Who knows if we'll have another chance?"

"Who knows if we'll have *this* chance," I muttered. But I recognized the look in Tania's eyes. There was no point in arguing with her. She'd just go without me— and I didn't want to miss anything interesting. "Then let's go now and get these costumes off."

We told Mom we were heading downstairs. She nodded absently. "All right, I just have to talk to this one last person."

We slipped away, knowing she'd be a while. We passed Maggie and Lionel, who were giggling over something. I felt a pang of jealousy and told myself it was stupid. Tania paused. "Lionel, what's the stuff I use to get these off?"

He smiled at her. "Had enough, darling? I'll come down with you. I've just gotta get out of these wounds. They itch."

Maggie looked around. "The party is winding down. I might as well change too."

We all headed downstairs. It took me about thirty seconds to get out of my lab coat. I waited while Lionel helped Tania with her teeth. Pretty soon, she looked normal. Maggie had gone to the bathroom to change. Lionel started working on his own monster makeup, turning back into an average-looking guy with blond hair and beard, bald on top.

Tania and I exchanged looks. "I'll just head to the bathroom to rinse off my face," she said.

"Yeah, I'll, um . . . stop in the bathroom too," I said.

We slipped out as Lionel was peeling the bullet hole off of his forehead. "Come on, quick!" Tania hauled me toward the elevator. "I hope we don't meet anyone on our way up."

"Yeah, and what are you going to do about that guard?"

"Wait until his back is turned." She always had an answer for everything.

The elevator let us out in a little nook. We could hear voices nearby. We peered around the corner and saw a few party guests heading toward the main entrance. The guard stood across the room, hands clasped behind his back. He watched everyone as if he thought they might grab a painting or two on their way out.

"We need a distraction," Tania said.

"Right, I suppose you want me to go shove over a statue or set off an alarm or something," I said with a laugh. Then I saw the look in her eyes and groaned. I shouldn't even joke about stuff like that.

CHAPTER
4

f you talk to the guard and get him to turn his back, then I can sneak into the room—"

"Forget it," I said. "You're not going in there alone."

Tania glared at me, but she didn't say anything. I bet she was secretly glad. She acts like she can handle ghosts, but she can't. Something always goes wrong, like that blast of cold fear. Maybe I couldn't keep that from happening, but at least I could be around to help pick up the pieces.

She crossed her arms. "All right, then, what would you suggest?"

I thought a minute. We could wait around and hope something else distracted the guard. But if the party was dying down, Mom and Bruce might head for the elevator soon. "Let's pretend we're going back to the party. Maybe we can find something in there to help. We could point out something strange to the guard."

Tania nodded. We strolled past the guard and stopped in the doorway of the Sculpture Court. I looked for Mom and Bruce first. Fortunately they were busy talking to reporters across the room.

A few dozen people still milled around. Madame Natasha was showing off to a ballerina, an Egyptian pharaoh, and a guy in a vampire costume. He was kind of plump and red-faced, though, so he didn't make as good a vampire as Tania.

"Maybe we could get Madame Natasha to create a scene," I said. "She's good at it."

Tania wrinkled her nose. "I don't want to give her any clue to what's going on. Anyway, she's got a crowd around her."

"Yeah." I glanced around again. Mean Mick was standing by himself, shoveling food in his mouth. I remembered how he got me in trouble on our last shoot, on the steamboat. He caught me unscrewing some bolts on the paddle-wheel cover—for a good cause, of course—and totally humiliated me in front of everyone. I still owed him for that.

"Okay, look," I whispered to Tania. "Mick is always waiting for me to do something wrong. I'll make him think I'm up to something. But wait for me before you go back to the ghost!"

She nodded and moved behind a statue to wait.

I walked past Mick, close enough to get his attention. I stopped and peered at a statue. When I glanced at him, sure enough, he was watching me suspiciously.

I leaned closer to the statue, like I was going to touch it. From the corner of my eye I could see Mick puff himself up and start toward me.

"Watch it," he ordered. "Those are priceless works of art. Don't touch anything."

I shrugged. "I'm not touching anything. Anyway, what business is it of yours? It's not your job to guard these statues."

"It's every good citizen's job to prevent crime!"

I raised my eyebrows. "It's not a crime to look. And I don't have to listen to you. You're not a museum guard." I hoped he'd get the hint. If he went for my mother instead, we'd both be in trouble.

Mick took a step closer. "Listen, you. Everyone thinks you're so nice and smart. But I know better. You're just looking to cause trouble."

I stared at him. He was right about the last part, but I wondered why he thought everyone thought I was nice and smart. Did they really?

No time to wonder about that now. "I'm not doing anything, and you can't stop me." Okay, that didn't make sense, but who cared. "If a *museum guard* has something to say to me, then I'll listen."

At last he got it. He turned away with a *hrumph* and stalked toward the entranceway. I followed quickly, then ducked behind a group of chattering people.

A few seconds later, Mick came back in, practically dragging the guard. I kept my head down as Mick led the man over to where we'd been before. He was just starting to look around in confusion when I ducked out the entranceway with Tania close behind.

We dashed to the Arms and Armor room. Once through the door, I grabbed Tania to hold her back. I looked around to make sure we were the only people there. The suits of armor looked creepy now, like someone could have been inside, watching. It gave me a chill, even though I figured it was next to impossible.

I took a deep breath. We were alone. Just me, my sister, and a ghost.

Tania pulled against my arm. "Come on, Jon, let me go."

"Wait a minute. Can you see him from here?"

"Yes, he's in that doorway looking at us."

I stared at the doorway too, but of course I couldn't see anything. I'd stopped doubting Tania—but it still bugged me that she could see something cool and I couldn't. I looked back at her. "What does he look like?"

"He's young, hardly even a grown-up," she whispered. I guess she didn't want him to hear us talking about him. "Maybe nineteen or twenty. Brown hair, kind of long. Short beard. He's wearing a long tunic kind of thing over tights."

I glanced toward the doorway in disbelief. "Tights?"

"You know, hose, or whatever they were called. Like in the Middle Ages. And boots."

"All right, what's he doing?"

"He's standing there, and he looks kind of . . ." She squinted. "Well, kind of like he's ready to defend something. Like he's on his guard. I can't explain, it's just the way he's standing."

"All right, don't get too close, and try talking to him."

"Who made you boss?" Tania muttered. She took a few steps forward. I stayed close beside her, ready to grab her if anything should happen.

"Hello," she said. "My name is Tania. Who are you?"

I made myself turn to watch Tania's face instead of the doorway that looked empty to me. Her forehead wrinkled, and she bit her lip.

"What's the matter?" I asked.

"He's saying something, but I can't catch it." She took another step forward. She spoke louder and slowly. "My name is Tania. This is my brother, Jon. We want to help you. Can you tell us why you're here?"

I was looking toward the empty space again. I couldn't seem to help it. I was straining my ears, too, as if this time I might actually hear something.

A voice boomed. "Ha! I knew it."

CHAPTER
5

I staggered forward a couple of steps with a gasp and turned toward the voice behind me. Mean Mick stood with his hands on his hips, next to the museum guard.

Tania had spun around too, and we stared at them. My heart was pounding, and I gasped for breath. My brain tried to tell my body that it didn't have anything to be scared of, but my body wasn't listening yet.

"I knew you were up to something," Mick said. "Just what do you think you're doing in here?"

I swallowed a couple of times. "We're just looking around."

"Isn't that okay?" Tania asked with wide-eyed innocence.

Mick looked at the guard, obviously waiting for him to arrest us or something. The man frowned. "The museum is closed, except for the party, and it's almost over. You kids really shouldn't be in here now. What's so special about this room, anyway?"

My heart had gone back to normal, and my brain seemed to be working again. I decided that, for once, the easiest answer might be the truth. I looked right at the guard, ignoring Mick. "It's that story—you must have heard it. About something funny happening with a sword?"

The guard's face moved, but I couldn't figure out his expression. Then he nodded, once, slowly, like he wasn't going to admit too much.

"We just wanted to see for ourselves. See if there was anything here."

"That's the most ridiculous thing I've ever heard!" Mick blustered.

Tania smiled at him. "Are you saying you don't believe in ghosts and things like that?"

He stopped with his mouth open. I remembered Maggie saying once that you didn't have to believe in order to work on the show. But she let Bruce and everyone assume that she believed, because it was easier. Mick might want to do the same.

"We just love stuff like that," Tania gushed. "After all, we're with the *Haunted* TV show. Of course we're interested in anything strange."

"Well, you should try coming back during regular

museum hours, with your parents." The guard stepped back and gestured for us to leave the room. "Come on, now. The party's winding down, so you'll probably be leaving soon."

Tania gave me a pleading look, but what could I do? "Yeah," I said, "maybe we can come back tomorrow."

She sighed and nodded. As she walked past the guard, she said, "Thanks for being so nice about this. We didn't mean to do anything wrong."

He smiled at her. "That's all right. But it must be past your bedtime now."

She gave a little yawn. "I am pretty tired. Well, good night."

We met Mom and Bruce by the elevators. I waited for Mick to say something. He looked at Mom and opened his mouth, but she didn't even glance at him. Mick looked down at his feet and kept his mouth shut after that.

When we got down to the storage room, I slumped into a chair. I just wanted to be in bed. It seemed to take forever to get back to the hotel. Fortunately, everyone slept late. I won't claim I was the first one up, but for once I was out of bed before Mom called our room.

It was midmorning by the time we made it to the hotel restaurant. Maggie was there, finishing her coffee. She sat with us while we ate.

"Well, what do you want to do today?" Mom asked. "We have a few days to enjoy New York."

"You get to enjoy New York," Bruce said. "I have meetings."

Mom touched his arm. "You'll have some free time. We should try to go to a show one evening."

"Sounds great! I'd better run." I looked in the other direction while he kissed Mom. Then Bruce took off.

Mom turned to Tania and me. "It's a nice day. We could take the ferry out to the Statue of Liberty."

I looked at Tania. The ferry sounded good, but I knew what she wanted.

"Can we go back to the National Museum?" she asked.

"Sure, if that's what you want," Mom said. "There are lots of other museums in New York as well, you know. The American Museum of Natural History, the Museum of Modern Art, Ellis Island."

"But the National was so cool," Tania said, "and we hardly got a chance to see anything."

Mom looked at me, and I nodded. "Yeah, the National Museum would be good. I want to get another look at all that armor and stuff." I figured that would be a good excuse to get back to the right area.

Maggie grinned. "Why are guys always interested in

weapons? I'd love to hit the National myself. Mind if I join you?"

"Excellent!" The word popped out. I avoided looking at Tania. We didn't really want anyone else around when we tried to reach the ghost, and Maggie already seemed suspicious. But hey, we couldn't be rude.

"Mick was going back to the National today too," Maggie said. "He asked if I wanted to join him, but . . ." She shrugged. "I said I had to finish breakfast."

"I can't blame you," Mom said. "It's bad enough having to work with the man."

"He's not that bad," Maggie said.

We all stared at her.

She shrugged again. "I get tired of him, but he doesn't really mean any harm. He just has poor social skills."

For someone who didn't mean any harm, he sure caused enough of it. At least the museum was a big place. We should be able to avoid him.

We took a taxi up through Central Park. People were out enjoying the sunshine, in-line skating or throwing balls to their dogs. It looked like a fun place to wander. It felt funny to be going to a museum—by choice—on such a nice day. But a museum with a ghost was different.

We got our tickets at the big entrance hall. "What first?" Maggie asked. "I recommend the Egyptian section, and it's right off here."

I looked at Tania, figuring she'd want to get right to the ghost area. But she chewed on her lip a second, and then nodded.

"Egypt, it is," Mom said.

As we headed toward that wing, Tania whispered to me. "We've got to ditch them before we get back to the ghost. Watch for a chance to slip away."

I sighed. I knew we had to do it, but I also knew we'd get in trouble. Or rather, I would—being the oldest, somehow things were always my fault.

We wandered through rooms all crammed with stuff from Egypt, from tiny pots and statues to real mummy cases and whole chunks of walls. It'd take a year to actually look at everything in there. But the mummies were really cool.

We spent about an hour going through the Egyptian wing. Then we came out into this huge room with a little stone temple. Maggie and Mom wandered toward it, chatting. Tania grabbed me. "Come on, this is our chance!"

She pulled me through a doorway. For a few minutes we just hurried along, with no idea where we were going. "This place is huge," I muttered. "We could be lost for hours."

At last we found a map in a stairwell. It got us going in the right direction, though everything seemed a lot farther away than it should be. A few little rooms on the map took us five minutes to get through. I wondered what Mom and Maggie were doing. They'd surely noticed by now that we were gone.

"Now I know where we are!" Tania said. I recognized the room with the statues. A lady was lecturing to a tour group. For the first time, I realized how crowded the museum was. How could we talk to the ghost with people all around?

We pushed into the Arms and Armor room. A female guard stood by the door, no one we'd seen before. A dozen people wandered around. One guy was in the alcove with the ghost sword.

Tania folded her arms and tapped her foot. I shrugged and took a closer look at the armor. Some of it was really fancy, with pictures etched into the metal. I could understand the images of lions or men holding swords. But why would anyone want armor with flower designs, or fat, naked babies?

The armor looked bulky and heavy, like it'd be hard to move in it. But I realized I was half a head taller than most of the suits. I guess people were short in the old days. "Hey Tania, is the ghost just a little guy?"

She stared at me. "Why does it matter?"

I shrugged. It didn't really, I just didn't like not knowing things. It made me feel stupid.

I wasn't really listening when the announcement came over the loudspeaker, but I caught my name. We were supposed to meet our party at the information booth. Yep, we'd been missed. Mom would be frantic.

The tour group came in and gathered by the mounted armor. Most of the other people in the room wandered closer to listen. Tania grabbed me and pulled me toward the little side room. I watched where she was looking, trying to figure out where the ghost was. I'd learned from experience you didn't want to run into one of those guys accidentally.

I tried to picture him from Tania's description, but the details, especially his face, were a blur. Maybe that's how he really looked, though—he was a ghost, after all.

"I'm sorry we had to leave last night," Tania said. "We're your friends, and we'd like to help you." She listened for a minute, frowning, then turned to me. "We have a problem."

Why wasn't I surprised? "What?"

"I don't think the ghost speaks English."

CHAPTER

6

I closed my eyes for a second. "Any idea what language he's speaking?"

She bit her lip and looked toward the sword. "French? It could be Spanish, but I don't think so. It doesn't sound like German or Russian, anything kind of throaty like that. I guess it could be Italian or something. I'm not sure I'd be able to tell. Do you know any French at all?"

I racked my brain. "Déjà vu? Croissant? Latte?"

She rolled her eyes. "Knock it off, this is serious! Anyway, I think 'latte' is Italian."

"The sword was supposed to be French, I guess. We should have expected this." I looked back toward the ghost, wishing I could see or hear him, even if I didn't understand him. But no, everything had to go through Tania.

I sighed. "Look, we'd better get back to Mom before

she has this place swarming with security guards looking for us," I warned.

She grumbled, but what else could we do? We made our way quickly through the museum, not talking much.

A French ghost knight. Wild. This was our coolest ghost yet. Even better than the steamboat pilot, and way better than the dead lady wailing over her missing husband. But hardly the kind of thing we could deal with secretly, when neither of us spoke French. I knew Tania would be disappointed.

I glanced at her as we headed down the big main staircase. "So I guess you don't get to help this ghost."

"What do you mean? We have to try!"

"Tania, you can't even talk to him. What are you supposed to do?"

"I don't know!" She sighed and shook her head. "You didn't see him. He's practically still a kid. And he looked so confused."

"I thought you said he looked defensive."

"Yes, but confused, too—like he didn't know what he was defending against."

"I know how he feels," I muttered, thinking of the times I'd had to defend Tania against an invisible ghost.

"He doesn't belong here. He must have come with the sword. Now he's stuck here, in the middle of the museum, in the twenty-first century. He's lost."

"And you have to help him." I sighed. "Couldn't you just rescue kittens or something?"

I spotted Mom by the information desk, eyes scanning the crowd. When she saw us, she cried out and rushed over. After the hugging, the scolding began. "Where have you been? You two know better than to wander off! I was so worried!"

When she finally paused for breath, Tania did her helpless, innocent act. "We're so sorry, it's my fault! I just went around a corner to look at something, and then got all mixed up. This museum is so confusing! I thought we were going back to you, and the next thing I knew, we were in, like, modern art or something."

"Well, don't do it again! From now on I want you in my sight at all times."

I tried not to groan aloud. Mom panics easily, ever since our little sister died. I guess I can understand why, but it sure is a pain. "Look, Mom, I'm thirteen. Tania's eleven. We're all right on our own for a few minutes. I mean, I'm sorry you were worried and didn't know where we were. But we would never leave the museum without you. It's not that big a deal."

"It is to me!" She put a hand on her chest and took a deep breath. "I know I worry. I can't help it. I just don't want anything to happen to you."

Tania gave her a hug and asked, "What could possibly happen to us here in the museum?"

I remembered the night before and was glad I didn't have to answer that one.

Maggie joined us. "Everybody okay?"

"Just great," I said. "Can we get some lunch?"

Maggie laughed. "Definitely normal. We can go downstairs."

The cafeteria was self-service, so we split up to find the things we wanted to eat. My stomach grumbled at the smells of grilled chicken, hamburgers, and pasta. Tania grabbed a yogurt and hissed at me, "We need to find someone who speaks French!"

"Yeah, okay." Like *that* would be easy.

As we headed for a table, I said casually, "Hey, Maggie, do you speak any foreign languages?"

"I can say 'hello' in five different languages. Does that count?"

I wondered what languages, but Tania interrupted. "Do you know anyone who speaks French?"

Maggie smiled slowly. "As a matter of fact, I do. He's right over there."

We all turned to follow her gaze. Mean Mick sat across the room, alone, eating a hamburger.

CHAPTER 7

"He was actually a languages major, with a minor in European history," Maggie said. "Fluent in French and Spanish, and I think he has some Italian or German or something."

"That's right," Mom said. "I asked Bruce once why on earth he hired Mick as the show's researcher. Bruce said Mick had good research skills, and you never knew when foreign languages might come in handy. Though I don't think we've needed them yet."

"You know . . . ," Tania said, "we really should go over and say hi. It's only polite."

"You go," Mom and I said at the same time.

Tania pouted. "Come on, Jon, what are you afraid of?"

"He hates me."

"He's just jealous," Maggie said.

I kind of laughed. Why would anybody be jealous of me, especially a grown-up?

"No, I mean it," she said. "You're everything he wasn't growing up."

I stared at her. "I'm what?"

She shrugged. "You're, well, likable. Friendly, out-going, popular."

"I'm not *popular*."

"You have friends, right?"

"Sure, I've got friends. But I'm not one of the popular kids or anything."

"What do you want to bet Mick didn't have any friends in school? Still doesn't. Making friends doesn't come naturally to him, and nobody ever taught him good social skills." Maggie shrugged. "I admit, he's sometimes hard to like. But I mostly feel sorry for him."

I thought about that for a while. I can't say it totally changed how I felt about Mick. I pretty much still thought he was a jerk. But it was interesting. "You know everything."

She laughed. "Except French. For that, you'll have to go to Mick."

"What's all this about French, anyway?" Mom asked.

"Oh, I just heard someone talking upstairs, and wondered about something he said." Tania jumped up. "Come on, Jon, let's go say hi to Mick."

I looked at Tania. She gazed back at me with the big, pleading eyes. I know that look, and it doesn't work on me. But I also knew she'd give me grief for the rest of the day if I didn't help her. Besides, I wanted to know what the ghost said too. "Okay, let's go."

She bounded across the room, and I dragged after her. Mick looked up at us. "Oh, hi."

"Hey!" Tania chirped. "Are you enjoying the museum?"

"Sure." Mick looked and sounded like Eeyore. But at least he wasn't trying to get me in trouble—yet.

"We have a question for you." Tania sat down at his table. "I heard someone talking upstairs, and I think it was French, and I wanted to know what he said. Maggie said you speak French."

"That's right." Mick started to look interested. "I have a master's degree—"

Tania interrupted before he could get into his bragging. "That's so cool! So can you tell me what something means?" She concentrated for second, then rattled off something I couldn't understand at all.

Mick frowned. "Say it again."

Once she did, Mick said, "Making some adjustments for mistakes, it sounds like, 'I will protect the sword for my Lord.' Where did you hear that?"

"Protect the sword . . . ," Tania said. "Who would do

39

that? I mean, whose job would it be to protect the sword for someone else?

"The *écuyer*," Mick said. "The literal translation is, 'shield bearer.' The word 'squire' comes from it. A squire was someone training to become a knight, and he worked as a knight's assistant."

"You mean he worked for one particular knight?" Tania asked.

Mick nodded. "He'd help the knight put on his armor. He might follow him to battle, carrying his extra weapons."

"Ah!" Tania's face lit up.

"The rest of the time, he trained to be a knight himself—practicing with weapons, learning good manners, stuff like that." Mick frowned. "Where did you hear all this, anyway?"

I made a face at Tania, trying to warn her to be careful. Mick was suspicious enough from last night.

"Some people were talking about a painting," she said. "I was just wondering." She chewed on her lip for a minute. "So if I asked you how to say something in French, you could tell me?"

"Sure, I guess."

"You are so nice!" Tania squealed. Mick actually blushed. "Wait—I'd better get some paper so I can make a note." Tania popped out of her chair and bounced back to Mom.

Mick and I looked at each other. I couldn't think of anything to say.

He sighed. "I guess you guys are having a good time."

"Yeah, it's okay." I really wanted to get out of there.

Mick fiddled with his napkin and looked like he was going to say something else. Fortunately, Tania came skipping back.

"Okay." She sat down and spread out a piece of notebook paper. She tapped the pencil against it. "What's the word for 'knight,' or 'lord'?"

Mick told her. She sounded it out a couple of times, and made a note on the paper. Then she asked about "dead" and "it is time to go." By the time she got to "your duty is over," Mick was staring at her.

"What do you want with all this stuff, anyway?"

Tania folded up her paper. "It's for . . . a story I'm writing. A project for school, about that painting I saw. I thought it would be cool to have actual French, since it was a French painting." She jumped up. "Well, thanks. Bye!"

I glanced at Mick, shrugged, and followed Tania.

As we crossed the room, she edged close to me

and whispered, "Now we just have to get back to the ghost!"

Sure. Easy. Find an excuse to go back up there, get rid of Mom and Maggie *again*, talk to a ghost in a language we couldn't speak, and then . . . who knew what would happen?

CHAPTER

8

Mom and Maggie were just finishing their sandwiches. "Ready to go?" Tania chirped.

She looked at me and I took my cue. "Um, can we do the weapons next?"

They agreed and started cleaning up the table. Tania folded her piece of paper into smaller and smaller squares. "You know what? We should ask Mick to join us."

Mom started to groan, then quickly covered it up. "That's a very nice thought, dear. Maybe he won't want to, though." She glanced at Maggie, who shrugged.

They looked at me, and I shrugged too. I knew Tania wanted her translator close by, but I was afraid she'd get more than she bargained for. It was going to be hard enough to do this with Mom and Maggie around.

Tania beamed. "Great!" She skipped back across the room to collect Mick.

They came back, and we all looked at each other awkwardly. Then Mom said brightly, "Well! Let's go."

We made our way through the medieval section without saying much. Finally Maggie asked Mick some question and got him talking. Tania edged closer to me. "You have to distract them while I talk to the ghost."

I didn't like it. Bad things tended to happen when she faced ghosts alone. Actually, they tended to happen when we faced them together, too. But at least then I knew what was going on.

Still, I couldn't think of any way for us both to get away from the others again. At least I could stay nearby, within shouting distance.

We went into the main Arms and Armor room and looked at the mounted soldiers. Tania fidgeted, giving me quick looks. I tried to think of a way to distract everyone else.

One of the side rooms was labeled EUROPEAN FIRE-ARMS. "Hey," I said, "does anyone know when they first made guns?"

Nobody did, of course.

I pointed at the side room. "Maybe it says in there."

Tania hung back as we went toward the alcove. The little room was small enough that it seemed crowded, even without Tania. Maybe no one would notice that she hadn't joined us. We read the labels with the guns, and I made some dumb comments just to keep people distracted. I hardly knew what I was saying. My mind was with Tania, facing the ghost alone.

The seconds seemed to limp by like hours. How long would she take? What if the ghost got angry or upset again? I listened for a scream or a thump—any sound of trouble. I imagined finding her passed out, or frozen.

I glanced around the room, restless. Wait, where was Mick?

I stuck my head out the doorway. Mick was walking across the big room, toward the alcove with the sword—and Tania.

"Mick!" I darted after him.

He whipped around.

I ran up to him. "What are you doing?" I was almost shouting, hoping Tania would hear.

"What? Oh. Nothing." He shrugged and shuffled his feet. Finally he muttered, "I just wanted to get a look at that sword everyone was so interested in."

I gaped at him. I'd been sure he was trying to spy on Tania. "Oh. Right. Yeah, it's pretty cool."

Maggie and Mom came up beside us. "What's going on?" Mom asked. "Why did you run off?"

My mind spun. "Um. I just realized that . . . Tania . . . wasn't in the room with us." Let her get in trouble for once. "I figured I'd make sure she hadn't wandered off too far." I was still talking too loudly. She had to hear me, but she hadn't appeared. Maybe she was hurt!

I leaped toward the ghost room. "Mick wanted to see that funny sword!" I'd have a few seconds before anyone else caught up.

As soon as I passed the doorway, the cold hit me. Tania was leaning against the wall, her arms wrapped around herself.

"You okay?" I whispered.

She nodded. "It's not working. He keeps repeating the same thing, about the knight."

Mom, Maggie, and Mick crowded in the room, exclaiming about the cold. Tania whispered, "He was getting upset."

"Yeah, I guess so," I said, shivering. I grabbed her arm and pulled her back out the doorway. She looked pale, almost blue. "I don't want you trying to talk to any ghost without me again," I said.

That got some color in her cheeks. "You're not in charge!"

Mom joined us. "I wish you two wouldn't keep running in and out! You're making me dizzy."

"Sorry," I said. "It was just so cold in there."

"It sure was," Mom said. "I wonder if there's anything to these strange stories."

Tania stared at her a moment. "Bruce should do a show about it!"

Mom frowned. "I don't know. There probably isn't enough here for whole show. Just a falling sword and a cold room. Not too exciting."

"But he could investigate and stuff! Whose sword it was, and all that."

Mom smiled at her. "I'll mention it, honey. But we probably need more to work with."

Maggie and Mick came out of the alcove. Mick was frowning, as usual. Maggie gave us a quick smile. "Ready to move on, gang?"

I was ready to get out of the museum, maybe see some sun, but Mom wanted to see these sculptures by a guy named Rodin. They were good, I guess, but my brain was tired of art.

I sat on a bench in the middle of a room, where I could look around without moving. Tania went up to Mick, but I couldn't hear what she was saying. He said something back. When I saw his scowl, I jumped up to join them.

"Is this some kind of a joke?" he asked. "Are you kids pulling a prank on me?"

"We would never do that!" Tania said, doing her cute-little-girl act. Of course, Mick is probably the one person in the world who wouldn't buy it.

"So why are you asking all these questions? Where did you get these phrases, about protecting the sword and duty to the knight?"

Tania gazed at him helplessly. I couldn't think of a good excuse either.

He glanced toward Mom and Maggie, across the room. "You're trying to get me in trouble," he hissed. "Your mom already hates me. What have you been telling her?"

"Nothing!" Tania said. "We haven't—we aren't."

Mick glared at me. I held up my hands. "I haven't said anything about you. But you know, maybe we don't have to. Mom sees the way you treat us."

Mick actually looked confused. "What do you mean?"

"You're always trying to get me in trouble! Watching everything I do, tattling. Why do you hate kids so much?"

Mick stared at me. "I don't hate kids."

I snorted. "Oh, so it's just me, then. Come on, Tania." I turned and walked away.

We flopped on the bench and watched Mick leave the room, his head down.

"You'd better avoid him," I said.

"But I don't know anyone else who speaks French!" Tania sighed. "We need a way to spend more time here."

"Yeah. Only thing is, Mom is going to get suspicious if we want to keep coming back here. There's, like, a billion other things to do in New York. Why would we want to spend every day in this one place?"

"If we could just get Bruce to film here, we'd have plenty of reasons to hang around that room."

"Right. Only he won't, without more evidence. Do you want to tell them you saw a ghost there?"

She sighed. "You know I can't."

Tania got the look I knew too well. She was coming up with a plan. "I can't," she said slowly. "But we know someone else who would love to claim she saw that ghost."

"Who . . . oh, no." I covered my face with my hands and groaned. "First Mick. And now you want to work with Madame Natasha."

CHAPTER
9

Fortunately Madame Natasha was staying in our hotel. Did I actually say fortunately? I never imagined that I'd want to see The Fraud.

When we got back from the museum, Tania and I got rid of Mom by saying we wanted to rest, and went to Madame N's floor. She didn't answer our knock. We lingered in the hallway, debating whether or not to leave a note. Turns out we didn't have to, as the creature herself stepped out of the elevator. She was dressed in her usual billowy clothes, with too much makeup.

"We need to talk to you!" Tania hissed.

Madame Natasha raised an eyebrow, like she didn't trust us—which I guess shows she's not as dumb as she looks. "Come in my room. I've just been at the Manhattan Psychic Research Center. Fascinating people, very interested in my work."

She took the only chair in the room, and Tania and I sat on the bed. I let Tania do the talking, since it was her crazy idea. She took a deep breath. "The thing is, we found a ghost. At the museum."

Madame Natasha frowned. "What kind of ghost?"

"Did you hear about that sword? It's new, and it's been falling and things."

"Oh, yes. Someone was joking about it at the party, asking if I thought it was a ghost."

"But it isn't a joke!" Tania said. "We went to see it, and there's a ghost there."

"Really." The eyebrow went up again. "What kind of ghost?"

"He's a squire, from France."

Madame Natasha's fingers drummed the arm of her chair. "And what's he doing here, in a museum?"

"I guess he's still trying to protect the sword."

Madame N sat up straighter, and her eyes glittered. "A ghost knight, how exciting."

"No, no," Tania said. "He's not a knight, he's a squire. He worked for a knight, like an assistant."

Madame Natasha waved this away. "A knight sounds more dramatic."

Tania jumped up. "We're not doing this to sound good! We want to help the ghost."

"Of course, of course." Madame Natasha motioned Tania to sit down again. "My dear, you know I want to help the ghost. Of course that comes first."

Tania stared at her for a minute, then sat down. "Okay. The sword would have belonged to a knight, and it would have been the squire's job to take care of it for him."

"You spoke to him then? What exactly did he say?"

Tania clasped her hands. "See, that's the thing— he doesn't speak English. Only French. Do you speak French?"

Madame Natasha hesitated, like she didn't want to admit there was anything she couldn't do. Finally she said, "Very little. I studied it in high school, years ago."

"Well, I don't speak French either," Tania said. "I got Mick to translate a few words. That's how I figured out squire, and knight, and something to do with duty and the sword."

Madame Natasha nodded slowly. "So the ghost had a duty to the knight, and he didn't fulfill it, so he's still trying."

Tania flopped back on the bed. "And we have to help the squire finish his business."

"But he can't ever fulfill his duty now, right?" I said. Madame Natasha looked at me like a piece of furniture had started talking. "He's protecting the sword because that was his job," I explained. "So what does he want now? What would let him stop doing that job?"

"Maybe he needs to give the sword back to the knight," Tania said.

"Great," I grumbled. "Even if the knight is a ghost, he's obviously not here. I don't see how we can find him if he's back in France or wherever. And if the knight did become a ghost, he and the squire could have sorted this all out years ago. The knight must be dead and gone."

"In that case, the knight doesn't need the sword anymore, so we have to convince the squire of that." Tania clasped her hands and gazed at the fake psychic. "We need more time at the museum. Do you think if you told Bruce you saw the ghost, he'd do a show at the museum?"

Madame Natasha smiled. "I'll make sure of it."

We left her, and I guess she got to work. Mom was frowning when she came to get us for dinner. "Bruce won't be joining us. Apparently Madame Natasha came to him with some story about a ghost, and he's trying to arrange a shoot. He wants to do it right away. I told him we could plan it for later in the season, but once he gets an idea in his mind . . ." She shook her head. "Anyway, we're on our own this evening. I'd wanted to go to a play. There's a place where you can get half-price tickets last minute."

Tania and I exchanged glances. "We can still go," Tania said. I nodded. Mom looked disappointed about Bruce, and I felt a little guilty. We were screwing up her vacation. Mine too, of course, but I was getting used to that. The least we could do for Mom was whatever she wanted for the evening.

Mom hugged us. "You are such good kids!"

If only she knew.

Turns out Bruce couldn't get things organized overnight. We had one day of touring with Mom before they got set up. We spent it mostly in Central Park, with the zoo and a boat on the lake. The following morning, everyone headed to the museum. Once we told Mom it was okay for her to work, she got into it. But with all the people around, Tania and I couldn't do much but hang back and watch.

First Bruce interviewed a few of the museum employees. The ones who had put the sword into the display described how it had kept falling. They just explained what they had done to build and adjust the holders, and what had happened. They weren't making any claims that a ghost was responsible. I wondered if Bruce would even use that footage, or if he'd think it was too boring.

Meanwhile, Madame Natasha was busy practicing French phrases with Mick. When Tania and I wandered near, he gave us a long look. I decided maybe we'd be better off somewhere else.

"All right, Madame Natasha is up next!" Bruce called out.

Tania fidgeted. "I need to be there to hear what he says! She won't know what's happening."

"Yeah, we should have thought of that earlier."

No way could we hide in that little side room. They hardly had space for the cameraman, the camera, and whoever they were filming.

Stephan, the cameraman, stepped into the big room. "It's getting cold in there. I'm afraid the camera will start fogging up."

I glanced at Tania, and then pushed my way toward Bruce. "Hey, you could move the sword out here. You'd have a lot more room. The ghost is supposed to go where the sword goes, right?"

Bruce and Stephan looked at the museum employees. They held a quick, whispered conference and then said, "All right, give us a few minutes."

"I'm hungry," I said to no one in particular.

Mom overheard and glanced at her watch. "We should order up some sandwiches. I'll take care of it."

"I'll give you a hand," Lionel said. He leaned forward and said in a stage whisper, "Our little psychic doesn't want my help with her makeup. I'd be embarrassed to have people think I had anything to do with that face, anyway." They headed out.

Tania nudged me. "Come on, let's go see the ghost."

"You can see the ghost," I grumbled. "I can't see anything."

But I followed her as she edged her way toward the little room. As we stepped through the doorway, I noticed the cold. "*Brrrr*. Does that mean something? Is he getting worked up about all this?"

Tania cocked her head to one side, staring at empty space. "He does look anxious. He's pacing back and forth. He probably doesn't understand what's going on. I wish I could explain."

"Yeah, me too," I said, edging back toward the doorway. I didn't want a freaked-out ghost wandering through me by accident.

"Maybe I should ask Mick—"

"Forget it," I snapped. "He's already suspicious. For someone who doesn't want the world to know her secrets, you're not very careful."

Tania glared at me. "I'm just doing what I have to do."

"Okay." I glanced over my shoulder. "Now what you have to do is stay out of the way and let the Madame do her thing. Who knows, maybe it will even work."

A guy with dark hair and glasses pushed past me into the room. He was wearing white gloves and held a key in his hand. Tania and I watched him open the case.

He reached a hand in for the sword. Beside me, Tania moved forward and opened her mouth. I grabbed her arm.

The man's hand closed on the sword hilt. The air seemed to swirl, like a cyclone gathering energy.

Tania bit her lip. It didn't matter what she saw. She couldn't say anything now.

CHAPTER
10

A blast of cold ripped through the room.

I staggered backward. I heard a thud and a yell. The cold blinded me, as if my eyeballs froze.

Then I was on my knees, gasping for breath.

A hand grabbed my shoulder. I looked up, and Maggie's face swam through the fog. "Are you all right?"

I nodded. She turned away and knelt beside Tania, who was crumpled on the floor. I crawled toward them.

Maggie helped Tania sit up. My sister blinked and mumbled something. The pain in my chest eased.

Other people were running around. I wondered what had happened to the museum employee. I didn't feel like standing up yet, but I leaned through the doorway of the sword room. The guy was slumped back against the wall, gasping.

Someone helped him up and out of the room. Waves

of cold and anger kept spilling through the doorway. I struggled to my feet and backed away.

"Maybe we shouldn't try to move that sword after all," someone said.

"Are we going to let a ghost push us around?" another voice demanded.

"What ghost? I don't believe in them, and I'm not about to start now."

Another museum employee got in Bruce's face. "Is this some kind of hoax? We had your word that you wouldn't try anything funny."

"We didn't do anything! We're legitimate researchers—"

People started arguing about what had happened. You could feel the tension begin to boil.

My heart raced as energy ran through me. I wanted to fight, run, or yell. But mostly fight. I looked at Madame Natasha. "Maybe you should try out your French phrases right now."

She glanced at Stephan. "But the camera isn't set up yet."

"Oh, for—" I clenched my fists to keep my hands from strangling her. I stomped over to Mick, who was hanging back across the room. "You're the French expert. Go talk to the ghost!"

Mick gaped at me. "But I can't see ghosts!"

"You don't have to see it to talk to it. Just tell it to calm down!"

Mick looked around wildly. No one came to his rescue. They were too busy arguing. The museum guy shoved Bruce. Maggie leaped between them, her face twisted with rage.

My anger faded, replaced by sick fear. "We have to do something now!"

Mick walked toward the sword room with a look on his face like he was going to the dentist. He paused at the doorway, hunching against the cold wind. French poured out of his mouth.

The wind eased. Mick talked on.

My heart slowed. I realized my shoulders were knotted up, and loosened them. The anger and fear hadn't reached this end of the room. I took a step forward, then stopped. I wanted to get in there and help people, but I also wanted to stay back where it felt safe.

Voices calmed. The anger seemed to fade from the room. I started across slowly. The air had stilled. It still felt chilly, but not painfully so.

I crossed to Tania, and she stared back at me. "It was the ghost making people angry!" she whispered.

I felt kind of queasy. I liked to think I was in charge of myself. It was the only thing in the whole world I thought I could control. But had I been controlled by a ghost instead, taking on his emotions? Was that the only reason I'd yelled at Mick, pushed him around?

"What on earth is going on here?"

I whipped around to see Mom staring at the milling crowd. Bruce bounded over to her. "We had a manifestation! Mr. Fields went to take the sword out of the case and got blasted! You should have felt the energy in this room."

"Goodness, is everyone all right?" Mom's gaze landed on us. "Kids! Are you all right?" She hurried over. "I shouldn't have let you come. I never imagined—"

"Oh, Mom," Tania said, "we're fine! We were hardly even close enough to feel it."

"I don't want you here if it's going to be dangerous. This kind of thing never used to happen—"

"It was nothing," I said. "No one was hurt. It was just interesting. It's too bad you missed it." In reality, relief that she'd missed it made my legs go weak. If she had witnessed that in person, we wouldn't get anywhere near the museum again. Now if only everyone else would keep calm about it.

"I can't believe we missed all the fun!" Lionel said. "I hope these sandwiches are worth it." He winked and handed me one.

"You didn't get that on film?" Bruce asked Stephan. The cameraman shook his head. "I'd just moved the camera out here. I tried to film once things started happening—I might have gotten the very end of it, but I'm not sure."

Mick's plaintive voice came from the doorway. "Can I stop now?"

Maggie smiled at him. "You did great. I'm not sure what exactly you did, but it seems to have worked."

Tania darted over and whispered something to Madame Natasha. The fake psychic cleared her throat to get everyone's attention. "The ghost said—" She rattled off something that I guess was supposed to be French.

Mick stared at her, his forehead wrinkled. "What?"

Tania muttered something at her side. Madame Natasha repeated the foreign sentence, a little different this time.

"Oh," Mick said. "You probably mean—" He said something that sounded almost the same, but a lot more French. "That means, 'I will protect my Lord's sword until he can claim it.' Interesting, it's an old-fashioned way of speaking and—"

No one was listening to him. "Fascinating!" Bruce said. "Let's get some of this on film. What about the sword—no, we'd better leave it." He shoved people around until Stephan had the camera shooting in the doorway, Madame Natasha was in with the ghost, and Mick was out of camera range next to Stephan.

Mick coached Madame Natasha in how to say things like, "We mean you no harm." Tania and I couldn't get anywhere near, and of course Madame N couldn't actually hear what the ghost was saying. She claimed he just kept repeating himself, and that was as good a guess as any.

"The camera's fogging up," Stephan said.

"It's getting really cold, too," Mick said. "I don't like it!"

"All right, we'd better stop for now," Bruce said. "I guess we don't want another incident." He sighed, and we could tell he wasn't too sure about that.

Stephan pulled the camera back, and Madame Natasha came out of the room. Bruce said, "Well, we got some good footage. Not enough for an hour though. We won't be able to use this unless we get something more—"

"A séance!" Madame Natasha exclaimed.

CHAPTER
11

She gazed around the room with a sly smile. "We can contact the dead knight through a séance. I'll pass on his message to the ghost. Perhaps with permission from his master, the squire will be able to move on."

People started discussing the idea. I edged closer to Madame Natasha. "Do séances actually work?" I asked.

"This is a great opportunity." She looked like she'd won a prize. "I'll contact the Psychic Research Center for their help." I noticed she hadn't actually answered my question. If she couldn't talk to ghosts, I don't know why she thought she could talk to dead people who weren't ghosts.

We had another day of touring with Mom before they got the séance arranged. We also had time to make a few whispered plans of our own. While Tania distracted Mom shopping for scarves at a street stand, I ducked into an electronics shop. I bought a miniature radio microphone and receiver. That way Tania could talk to Madame Natasha secretly.

The whole thing seemed crazy. Hopefully Tania could stand someplace where she could overhear the squire's ghost. She could relay what he was saying to Madame Natasha, who could repeat it out loud. Mick could then translate it. Kind of like playing "telephone," with a foreign language thrown in.

But what about the knight? If they managed to contact him, would he actually show up in person, like a ghost? If so, the squire could talk to him directly. If Tania could hear the knight, then *they* could play this game of foreign telephone.

My brain felt scrambled, thinking about it all. I decided that the chances of Madame Natasha actually contacting the dead knight were about a zillion to one, so I stopped worrying. But maybe we could at least find out more about the squire.

When we got to the museum, a bunch of new people were there. Madame Natasha introduced Bruce to the members of the Psychic Research Center. I figured all the so-called psychics would be like Madame Natasha, with too much makeup and goofy clothes. But they looked normal—well, at least in comparison to her.

Dan, a tall, skinny guy in his fifties, wore a suit and looked like a businessman. Julie was thin and pale, with straight brown hair, a brown button-up sweater, and a brown skirt. Dorothy was stocky, about sixty, with gray helmet hair and an English accent. Lionel was waving a face-powder brush at her and saying, "Just for the camera, dear," while she backed away.

The final guy was young, and looked like a college student. He had spiky black hair and hip black clothes that we'd been seeing around New York. His name was Andy. Someone whispered that he had made his reputation as a local street magician, but supposedly he was psychic too.

"Julie, Dorothy, and Andy will join Madame Natasha in the séance," Dan explained. "I'll be a neutral observer, taking notes for the Psychic Research Center."

He pushed his glasses up his nose and frowned at Bruce. "We're skeptical of séances at the center, but willing to try this as an experiment. I should warn you, we have very strict standards for what we accept as evidence of the occult. We do serious research, and we need to protect that reputation."

It seemed funny to me that anyone would do serious research about something like ghosts. I thought of my father, the scientist, who dismissed everything super-natural with a laugh. Of course, if you never do the research, you couldn't know what was true. Some people would claim ghosts existed, because they thought they'd seen one once. Other people would say those sightings were hallucinations or fantasies or lies. I was glad to know some people were taking this seriously, but weren't just believing everything they heard.

They set up the psychics around a folding table. "Can we get a tablecloth?" Bruce asked.

"Absolutely not," Dan said. "We need to be able to see underneath, to make sure nobody is bumping the table to cause noise or movement. I'm sure you know how many fake psychics in the past did that kind of thing and pretended it was the dead signaling. We want complete transparency here."

Bruce sighed. "It just looks so tacky." But since he dreams of being taken seriously by the scientific community, he let it go.

"We need the sword out here," Bruce said. "Mick, tell the ghost we're just moving the sword, and won't do any harm."

Mick grimaced, but did as he was told. At least I assume he did; I couldn't understand a word he said.

The museum employee looked jumpy when he went in to get the sword. I was close enough to feel the cold air coming out of the little room. The guy practically sprinted out, holding the sword out flat in both hands. Did he imagine he could outrun the ghost?

"What's the squire doing?" I murmured to Tania.

"Staying with the sword. He's really breathing down that guy's neck."

The employee hunched up his shoulders as he laid the sword across the folding table. He hurried away, shivering.

"The ghost is reaching for the sword!" Tania whispered. "He has his hand on the hilt."

"This should be interesting," I muttered.

Madame Natasha sat at the table, facing out into the room. Mick stood behind her, looking really uncomfortable. The other three psychics sat around the sides of the table with two cameras, one on either side.

Tania and I edged as close as possible to the group. Someone dimmed the lights and all the psychics joined hands.

Madame Natasha said, "We are here to contact the knight who owned this sword." She closed her eyes and threw back her head. "O, knight, speak to us from the other side! Come to us here!"

Dorothy, the older psychic, said, "What is the knight's name?"

Madame Natasha opened her eyes and glared. "I don't believe anyone knows his name."

"His squire would know," Dorothy said mildly. "You could ask him."

Madame Natasha's mouth dropped open, and I chuckled. I kind of liked this Dorothy.

Madame N went into her routine again. "O, squire who protects the sword, tell us your name!"

Nothing happened. Tania ducked her chin toward her collar, where the microphone was hidden. "You have to say it in French!"

Madame Natasha turned to Mick. "Translate, please," she snapped.

He looked around the room, and said something in French. Most people looked at the sword. I focused on Tania, as she whispered something into the microphone.

Madame Natasha said pompously, "He is Jesse Hector Dubar."

Mick frowned, then cleared his throat. "*Je suis* means 'I am.' He must have said 'I am Hector Dubar.'"

"Of course," Madame Natasha said smoothly. "And now, Hector Dubar, tell us the name of the knight you served."

Mick did his translation bit. Tania listened and then muttered something into the microphone.

Madame Natasha's eyes opened wide. She said in a

kind of rush, "Le Chevally Alain Gulden Servee Jay!"

"Quite a name," I whispered.

Mick said, "That means, 'I served the knight Alain Gulden.'"

"Very well," Madame Natasha said. "Let us begin. We want to contact the knight Alain Gulden." She rambled on awhile, about parting the veil and asking the knight to speak. She glanced over at Tania, who shook her head. Madame Natasha frowned.

"I can't help it," Tania whispered. "No one else has shown up!"

Dan was making notes on his clipboard. Dorothy waited quietly, with a slight smile. I think Julie was humming. Andy glanced around the room, frowning and restless.

Madame Natasha's eyes opened wide, and she stared at the air above the sword. "He is here!"

Tania stomped her foot. "He is not!" She spoke a little too loud, and Lionel glanced at her. At least Mick was too busy to tell us to keep quiet.

"I feel his presence," Madame Natasha said. "Alain Gulden, welcome!" She paused a moment, then added, "He asks why we have called him here."

"What language is he speaking?" Dan snapped.

"He is speaking in ideas, not in any language," Madame Natasha said. Clever.

"Yes, yes!" Julie said. "I can feel his presence!"

Andy scowled. "Nonsense, there's nothing there." Dorothy just smiled.

"Alain Gulden, your squire is here, still serving you faithfully," Madame Natasha said. "Will you give him permission to move on?"

"Wait a minute," Julie said, "ask him some questions first!"

"Am I supposed to translate?" Mick asked.

"Slow down," Dan said. "We need to get some evidence."

Madame Natasha frowned and looked around. Tania crossed her arms. "She'd better not think I'm going to help her! She's just faking."

Madame Natasha pulled her hands away from Julie and Dorothy, and laid them on the sword hilt. "Alain Gulden, here is your sword. Do you recognize it?"

Dan stepped forward. "Don't touch it. You need to keep your hands clasped."

Julie tried to grab one of Madame Natasha's hands on the sword. A couple of museum employees came toward the table. "Please don't handle the sword," one of them said. He reached forward to grab Madame Natasha's arm.

"Ha!" Tania said. I glanced at her. When I saw the glee on her face, I quickly looked back toward the table.

The sword started shaking. At first, it just looked like everyone was fighting over it. Then Madame Natasha and Julie cried out and jerked back their hands.

A second later, the room seemed to explode.

CHAPTER
12

People were yelling and screaming.

I tried to suck in air, but it seared my lungs with the cold.

I blinked my stinging eyes. Someone grabbed my arm. I shook my head, trying to focus.

"Come on, Jon!" Tania's voice sounded far away. "We need to do something."

I looked around. It was total chaos. Madame Natasha was standing by the table, babbling something I couldn't hear. Dorothy had pushed her chair back and was staring at the sword. Andy was grasping the edge of the table, and both he and it were shaking. Julie had her hands over her mouth.

Bruce leaped around, yelling and gesturing. Madame Natasha's voice rose over the din for a moment—"more dramatic adventures like these in my latest book"—as the cameras filmed every frantic second.

I saw Mom leaning against a wall, one hand to her chest, mouth open, blinking. I grabbed Tania and started dragging her to the back of the room. "Come on."

She pulled against me. "But I want to hear what the ghost is saying!"

"Do you want to hear what Mom will be saying if she catches us this close to the action? Because she will, in a second."

Tania froze, glanced around until she spotted Mom, and then hurried with me to the back of the room. By the time Mom recovered enough to look for us, we were standing innocently by the far wall.

She hurried over. "Jonathan! Titania! Are you all right?"

"Of course," we both answered.

Mom glanced back across the room and then to us again. "You should really—"

I cut her off before she could get going. "But what about you? Were you close enough to feel anything?"

"Yes, it was like being hit by an Arctic storm. But—"

"It looks like Bruce needs your help," Tania said. "He must be so excited about this footage."

Mom glanced back again. Bruce shouted, "Keep rolling! Everyone in your places. Give me a microphone."

Mom turned to us and opened her mouth to speak.

I said, "Better hurry. You know how things fall apart when you're not in charge."

Tania nodded. "They really need you."

Mom threw her hands up, blew out a breath, and hurried across the room. I sagged against the wall, just wanting a minute to rest.

"Close," Tania said. "Come on."

I groaned and followed her. We stopped by the central display of mounted armor, keeping a horse between us and Mom. They had things under control again. The three guest psychics were sitting around the table. They had edged back and were barely sitting close enough to touch each other.

Madame Natasha stood. "O, great knight! You have shown us your presence. Your faithful servant has waited for you across the centuries. Now give him permission to move on, to join you across the veil." She pressed her hands together and bowed her head.

"What's the squire doing?" I asked Tania.

"He's standing by the table, where Madame Natasha was sitting. He has his hands on the sword hilt. It looks like he's trying to pick it up, but he can't. He has his head down—he looks upset."

"Let's hope she doesn't set him off again."

"She's not saying the knight's name this time. She must figure that's what did it."

Madame Natasha lifted her head and opened her eyes. She raised her hands toward the ceiling. "The knight has given his permission! The squire may move on."

She turned slightly and smiled, like she was talking to someone we couldn't see. "You may go to your final resting place."

Tania ducked her head and hissed into the microphone. "He's not even looking at you!"

Madame Natasha kept smiling. "Your trials are over. Peace be with you."

Tania stomped her foot. "No! It isn't over. We're not done."

I shushed her. She turned on me. "But she's lying!"

"I know," I whispered. "But you can't accuse her in front of everyone. Keep your voice down."

I thought she was going to cry—or kick something. Possibly me. But she kept quiet while Madame N finished her act. "He says it is a relief to leave this weary world. He thanks me. He is fading . . . he has vanished."

Finally Mom called, "Cut!"

Bruce rushed up to Madame Natasha and pumped her hand. "Brilliant! Fabulous! This will make a great episode. And it's the best evidence we have yet. Just think—if you hadn't spotted this ghost at the party, we might have missed all this!"

I avoided looking at Tania. I knew she was fuming at that comment.

Dan, the Psychic Research Center guy, stepped toward Bruce, clipboard still in hand. Bruce grinned at him. "Amazing, wasn't it?"

Dan frowned. "It was certainly interesting, but I wouldn't call it proof of anything."

Bruce gaped at him. "What do you mean? That cold—the force of the wind—didn't you feel it?"

"Oh, I felt it. We will have to go over this room carefully. Please don't remove any of your equipment until we've had a chance to examine everything. Ask everyone to step to the far side of the room now. And don't let anyone leave until we've had a chance to search them."

Bruce's jaw dropped even further. "You're not suggesting that I faked this! Didn't you see the sword move?

"Unfortunately the team didn't maintain their positions. Someone may have been shaking the table."

The psychics clustered around. "I had my hands on the table, but I wasn't shaking it," Andy insisted. "It was shaking me!"

"It was the strongest manifestation I've ever seen," Julie said.

"But what did you really see?" Dorothy asked. "In my opinion, you're a bit too susceptible to suggestion."

77

"Are you claiming nothing happened?" Julie gasped.

Dorothy blinked owlishly. "Oh, something happened. But I agree with Dan. Whatever happened may have a rational, human explanation. It's not evidence of a ghost."

"I can't believe I let myself get talked into this fiasco," Andy muttered.

Dorothy raised her eyebrows. "As I recall, you begged to come along. I got the impression a little national TV exposure appealed to you."

Madame Natasha smiled. "I realize that it is hard for those who cannot actually see ghosts, the way I can, to believe in them. If your gifts are not as strong, it is easy to doubt. But I saw the ghost squire shimmer and fade, in ecstasy as he moved to the next world."

Tania groaned. "I can't believe her."

"What does the ghost think of all this?" I asked Tania.

"He's not paying any attention to them. He's given up trying to move the sword. He's sitting at the table, with his head in his hands. He looks so frustrated."

Him and everybody else, I thought. Irritation flowed through the room as people bickered. How much was normal, after the strange things that had happened—and how much came directly from the ghost? Would people be getting so worked up if it weren't for his influence?

Couldn't they feel the difference? But no, everyone just thought other people were being unreasonable.

Madame Natasha kept herself aloof, calmly denying any tricks and insisting she'd helped the ghost move on.

Tania pulled the microphone from her collar and threw it to the floor. "I can't stand it! She's ruined everything."

"She's made a mess, all right." I wanted to throw something too. "Aren't you used to it by now? The Madame always seems to come out on top."

"But don't you see? If Bruce thinks the ghost has gone on, there's no reason to film here anymore. The show will pack up, and we'll leave, and the poor squire will be stuck here forever."

I sighed. "Yeah. And that room will still get cold, and the sword will still fall out of its place. And no one will ever know why."

Tania looked at me with wide eyes. "That's it! We have to prove to Bruce that Madame Natasha is lying."

I pushed my hands through my hair. "Oh, right. Exactly how will we do that?"

"We have to get the ghost to do something. Something that proves he's still here!"

CHAPTER
13

D an insisted that all the *Haunted* staff head to the far side of the room. The museum employee put the sword back in its case. Tania said the ghost just followed along behind. Maybe he'd drained himself with all that emotion.

A couple of people I hadn't noticed before helped Dan search in the area where we'd been filming. I guess they were from the Psychic Research Center as well. We shuffled around, waiting, crammed in with the other TV show people. Lionel whispered something in Maggie's ear, and she giggled. I scowled at them, wishing I were the one making Maggie laugh.

"I have to get back over there and talk to the squire!" Tania hissed.

"What are you going to say to him?"

"I'll tell him—" Tania made a face. "I can't tell him anything. I have to get Mick to do it."

"Or learn French real quick."

Tania stuck out her tongue, and then turned a sunny smile on Mick. "You were so wonderful over there!"

Mick looked at his feet. "I felt stupid."

"Oh, no!" Tania gushed. "You sounded great. They couldn't have done it without you."

Mick shot a glance at Madame Natasha. "She went on all right without me."

"But you found out the squire's name—Hector Dubar. And the knight. Alain Gulden."

Mick nodded. "Good French names, appropriate for the time. If she faked that much, she did her research."

Lionel leaned over with a grin. "But if she'd done her research, she would have known that *le chevalier* and *servi j'ai* weren't part of the name."

Mick frowned at him. "You speak French?"

"Oh sure, I spent two years in Paris, studying theater. But my French is a little more, shall we say, colloquial?" He winked at Tania. "That means I know all the bad slang. Don't worry, Mick, I won't try to take your new job." He snickered and moved away.

Tania gazed at Mick like he was some kind of hero. "So what would you have said to the ghost if you could have talked to him directly?"

Mick shrugged. "I don't know. How's life?" He chuckled.

"I'd want to know more about that knight, Alain Gulden," Tania said. "Who he was, and why Hector Dubar feels so much loyalty to him. Don't you think that would be interesting?"

Mick nodded. "I love that kind of thing. I wanted to major in history, but my parents said it wasn't practical. I went into languages because I could still get some of the history and culture. My parents said it was all right, because I could always work as a translator."

Okay, logically I know the guy had to have parents. But somehow it still threw me to think of Mick as a kid being bossed around by his folks.

A triumphant shout made us all look across the room.

Dan was holding up the little microphone Tania had thrown on the floor. "And just what was this used for?"

Bruce crossed over to Dan. "It's a microphone. But not the kind we use. Where did it come from?"

"That's a very good question," Dan said suspiciously.

"You're not suggesting—" Bruce started to bluster. "We're a TV show! We have lots of microphones! It's perfectly normal."

"Ah, but you just said it wasn't one of yours!"

As they argued, Tania and I exchanged a look. She bit her lip. I shrugged. Too late to do anything about it now.

Bruce stormed back to our group, his hair messed up and his tie crooked. He muttered to Mom about the nerve of some people.

The psychic research people finished searching the room. Then they started on us. They used wands, like they do at the airport, to check for metal. They even did a quick patdown. I guess they were looking for anything we might have used to cause the cold and shake the table. But they were taking their investigations a little too far for my taste. At least they wouldn't find that microphone on Tania.

When I was finished, Tania dragged me over toward the doorway of the sword room. "Now is our chance!" she hissed.

She turned on the charm again. "Mick! Mick, come over here and finish what you were telling us. It's so interesting."

He shuffled over, blushing. Man, that guy fell for it easily.

"So, Mick, what else would you ask the ghost squire?"

Mick's forehead wrinkled. "I guess I'd want to know what it was like. How he felt about his life."

"How he felt about working for Alain Gulden?"

"Well, yes. But a squire didn't just work for a knight, like an employee for a boss. It was much closer, in most cases. Almost like a younger brother, or a son, being trained in the family business."

"And that's why this squire was so loyal to Alain Gulden?"

I figured Tania was trying to use the knight's name as much as possible, hoping to set off the squire. I realized if anything did happened, we'd want to make sure Bruce witnessed it.

The Psychic Research Center people had finished the searches, and were interviewing the psychics from the séance with tape recorders. I wondered where Madame Natasha had gotten rid of her radio receiver.

Bruce and Mom crossed the room. "I can't believe the indignity," Bruce mumbled, straightening his tie.

Mom patted his arm. "Honey, you know if you want the scientific respect, you have to play by the rules."

I waved to get their attention. "Hey."

"Oh, Jon," Bruce said, "I'm sorry you and Tania had to go through that."

"It's okay. But I want to ask you something . . . um, about the sword. Could you come in here for a second?" We squeezed past Tania and Mick. I gave Tania a look that said, *Hurry up*.

It was chilly in the sword room, but that didn't prove anything. I hoped Tania got a reaction quickly, because I had no idea what I was going to ask.

Bruce stared at the sword, with a moody frown. I could hear Tania. "Do you think that's why Hector Dubar stayed around? He was supposed to bring the sword to Alain Gulden in battle, but couldn't? He was probably killed before he could. Now he feels guilty that he didn't do his duty."

"It's a good guess," Mick said. "The knight might have been fighting with another weapon, like a lance, at first. And then called for his sword. Or maybe he broke or lost his first sword. It's possible that the knight even died because the squire didn't get him the replacement weapon in time."

"So how would you say that in French?" Tania asked.

Mick chuckled. "In French? Why does that matter?"

"Oh, I don't know, I just love to hear it. It's such a pretty language. And you have a beautiful voice."

I was glad Mick couldn't see me roll my eyes. Anyway, her trick worked. He stood just outside the door, talking in French. He spoke louder than he had been, showing off, I guess.

Bruce turned to me. "Sorry, what did you want to ask?"

"Well, it's just the sword . . ." I pointed at it. "With everything that happened, what do you think it really means?"

Bruce sighed. "I'm absolutely convinced that there was a ghost here. Maybe we don't have proof enough for that guy, but I know what I saw and felt, and I know we didn't fake it."

"Yeah, but if Madame Natasha really got rid of the ghost, then you're kind of stuck. There's nothing you can do now. Show's over."

He nodded sadly. "I guess I should have given her a little more guidance."

Mom snorted.

I stared at the sword. It seemed to wiggle. I heard Tania's voice, then Mick's again, in French.

"Look," I said. "Doesn't it look like the sword is moving?"

Bruce and Mom stepped closer. "Oh gosh," Mom said, rubbing her arms. "It's freezing again."

The sword was trembling in its holder, no doubt about it. "We've got to get the others!" Bruce said. "Get Dan!" But he just kept staring.

"But how will we prove anything?" Mom asked. "I'm afraid as soon as we turn our backs, it will stop."

The sword seemed to lift up a little. Then it came out of the holder. For a moment it hovered in the air. I could imagine a hand holding it, trying to raise it.

The sword clattered to the bottom of the case.

Mom squealed and put her hands to her mouth.

Bruce yelled something I didn't catch. I felt the cold building up, and the frustration.

I grabbed Mom and pulled her toward the doorway. I just had time to get between her and the ghost before the hurricane hit.

CHAPTER
14

Maybe the ghost was getting weaker, or maybe I was just used to this stuff now. It only took a few seconds before I recovered. Mom was sandwiched between me and Mick. I guess we'd run into him as we pushed out the doorway.

Tania stood nearby, grinning. Bruce was shouting in the sword room.

Mom started to wriggle, so I stepped back. It was still cold, but the wind had stopped. The frustration lingered.

Bruce stepped out of the sword room, his hair wild, shouting and waving. "Did you feel that? Did you see that? It happened again!"

Dan and his crew of investigators looked at us from across the room. "What happened?"

"Didn't you feel it? The cold wind! And the sword

fell!" Bruce stared at Dan, thirty feet away, and his shoulders sagged.

"I felt it suddenly get cold and windy again," Maggie said. "And I heard a clang." But she'd been near the doorway. I guess none of the cold made it across the big room.

The museum employee pushed forward. "If you've done something to the sword—"

"I didn't!" Bruce said. "How could I? It's in the case. What do you think I could have done?" He looked around at everyone, his eyes pleading. "It was the ghost, I know it was."

I was starting to feel bad for him. I looked at Tania. She bit her lip for a second, but she wasn't one to let a little guilt interfere with her plans. She said loudly, "But Bruce, Madame Natasha said that the ghost has gone on. She said she spoke to him, and saw him. *If* she was telling the truth, how could the ghost possibly be—"

Madame Natasha stormed over, glaring. "Nonsense! Of course I told you the truth." She gave a little laugh and looked around. "Children. Such imaginations."

Bruce said, "But she's right. If this wasn't the ghost, what was it? *Something* just happened. It felt the same as before."

Dan crossed the room to join us. "It is cold over here

again. But that just suggests some natural reason for the phenomenon we've been witnessing." He gave Bruce a look. "Or some man-made one."

"I didn't do anything!" Bruce wailed.

"We know you didn't," Tania said clearly. She lifted her chin. "I don't see how anyone could have faked everything that happened. So I think it was a ghost. And he hasn't gone on—he's still here."

Everyone turned to look at Madame Natasha. I could see her swallow. She was trapped. If she claimed the most recent cold, wind, and sword moving weren't caused by a ghost, then we'd lost all evidence that there ever *was* a ghost. But if she admitted the ghost was still here, she had to admit that she lied.

"Perhaps I was a little hasty," she said. "When I saw the ghost vanish, maybe he did not actually go on to the next world. He may have been hovering nearby, for reasons of his own."

"But you said he told you he was going on," Tania said.

Madame Natasha's glare could have set Tania on fire. Tania just returned it.

"Don't forget, I felt something too," Julie said.

Dorothy snorted. "You claimed you saw some blurry figure of a knight wearing long robes. But Ms. Natasha said the knight was wearing armor. And neither of you could give clear details that match with appropriate clothing of the time."

"Well, we're finished here," Dan said. "We'll have to go over the video evidence and type up the reports." He gave Bruce a cold look. "But I can tell you my initial impression. The show's methods are sloppy, and I have grave doubts that your supposed psychic has any special powers at all. I'm afraid *Haunted* will go on our list of 'not legitimate' organizations. When the report is finished, we will release it to the media, and post it on our website. I'll fax you a copy."

He started to pack up as Bruce and Madame Natasha yelled and pleaded.

I turn to Tania. "Satisfied?"

Her lower lip trembled as she watched Bruce. "At least we showed what a fake Madame Natasha is."

"Yeah." I didn't point out that since the psychic looked bad, the whole show looked bad. It was a little late now. Anyway, I couldn't say "I told you so," because I hadn't. Neither of us had thought this plan through.

We stood around while people argued and discussed and complained.

Tania looked into the sword room.

"Don't start anything now," I muttered.

Tania sighed. "Hector Dubar looks so sad. How can we help him?"

"Hey, this is your crusade. I'm just here to hold your sword."

Mom grabbed us and pulled us back. "Stay away from there. It's not safe."

"Oh, Mom," Tania said. "He wouldn't hurt anyone."

"You don't know that. We don't even know what it is, now."

"I mean, he *hasn't* hurt anyone," Tania said quickly. "I'm sure it's all right."

Mom shook her head. "We're not taking any chances. Anyway, as soon as they pack up the cameras, we can go."

"Go!" Tania wailed. "But what about the ghost? We haven't finished."

"I think we've had more than enough," Mom said. "This has been a disaster." She blinked a bunch of times, fast, like she was trying not to cry. Then she spun around and stumbled across the room, fumbling in her purse until she found a handkerchief.

"What are we going to do?" Tania wailed. "This is awful."

I felt sick. We'd screwed up big. I wasn't crazy about Bruce, but I hadn't meant to hurt him. And I didn't want Mom to suffer any. She'd had plenty of pain in the last few years.

I sighed and rubbed my hands over my face. "We'll make it up to them," I said. "We have to. Somehow."

Bruce shuffled over, head down, shoulders slumped. Tania grabbed his arm. "You're not really leaving? Just calling it quits?"

Bruce managed a thin smile. "It's the best thing we can do now. That report is going to hurt the show's reputation. We need to get out of here, burn the film, and pretend this never happened."

He took a deep breath and let it out. "It's over."

CHAPTER
15

Tania stared at him, looking as white as—okay, I'll say it: as a ghost. "You can't just give up!"

"But honey, what else can we do?" He shook his head. "It will take *Haunted* a long time to recover from this."

They both looked miserable. I wished we'd never started this, never found the ghost. We could have had a nice vacation. . . . But was not knowing really better? I realized that I'd just been tagging along after Tania, resentful that she could see the ghost and I couldn't. It was time to decide if this was my quest too. Time to help for real, or give up and get out.

"Look," I said, "is the show really a complete loss? You got some good footage, right?"

"We can't use any of that stuff with the séance," Bruce said.

"But what about earlier? You have the interviews

with the museum staff. The stories about the sword falling. And Stephan said he might have gotten something the first day, when that guy from the museum tried to move the sword and got blasted."

"Well, that's true . . . ," Bruce said.

"I bet you could still make a great show!" Tania said.

"You just need a little more footage," I said. "Get Mick in there talking to the ghost in French, and maybe you'll even get another, what do you call it, manifestation."

"Just don't let Madame Natasha do anything!" Tania said. "Without her, you'll do great."

"You said yourself, this is the best evidence you've ever had," I wheedled. "You can't just let it go. Who cares what those people think? This is your show."

Bruce gazed at the sword room and frowned. "Maybe . . . let me talk to your mom."

Mom and Bruce started discussing the options. Soon Maggie and the camera operators joined them.

Tania and I edged away. She grinned at me. "Perfect! Thank you, Jon."

I shrugged. "Maybe I bought us some more time. We still have to figure out what to do with the ghost."

I caught a glimpse of red from the corner of my eye, heading toward us. At first I thought it was Madame

Natasha's hair, but maybe it was really the fire shooting from her eyes. "How dare you!" she hissed. "You've
made me look like a fool."

"Well, you make it so easy," I said.

"We had a deal!" Madame Natasha's eyes glittered.
I resisted the urge to step back.

Tania thrust out her chin. "And you broke that deal!
I only told you about the ghost so we could help him.
You had to show off, and pretend you're so great, and
the show would have left the museum without doing
anything for the ghost."

"And now you see what you've done?" Madame
Natasha waved toward Bruce. "You've ruined his reputation along with mine."

"That's our problem." Tania's voice barely shook.
"And you aren't anymore."

Madame N leaned in closer. "That's what you think.
I'll see that *Haunted* takes the blame for this."

The chill I felt was worse than when the ghost
was going crazy. But I took a deep breath and looked
Madame Natasha in the eye. "Bruce is ready to forget
all about you. That's the best thing for you, now. Lay
low for awhile, and then go play your tricks someplace
else. People will forget this, if you let it go. But not if
you keep making a fuss."

Madame Natasha stared at me. I realized I was holding my breath. I let it out slowly, hoping she wouldn't notice.

"You're already on two shows this season," I added. "You've had your publicity. Don't cause us any more trouble, and we'll see that Bruce doesn't say anything bad about you in public." I didn't know if I could keep that promise, but I figured at this point Bruce would want to say as little as possible about his pet psychic gone bad.

My eyes were starting to water, trying to hold Madame Natasha's gaze. Tania said, "We're even now. You don't bother us, and we won't bother you."

I blinked at last, while Madame Natasha turned her glare on Tania. "I'll let this go—for now. But I won't forget it. We're nowhere near even."

She turned and stormed out of the room. I sagged, and wished I was closer to a wall, so I could lean against something.

"Phew!" Tania hugged herself. "I'm trembling. I'm glad that's over."

"I hope it is," I muttered. I took a deep breath and tried to shake off the mood. "Better forget about her, and figure out how you're going to help your squire."

We joined Bruce, Mom, and Maggie as they debated what to do next. The other employees waited nearby, listening.

"If you want to get taken seriously now," Maggie told Bruce, "you have to get serious about research. Find out who owned the sword. Its history, what happened to it, as much as anyone knows."

"Mick?" Bruce said, turning to him. "Is that possible?"

Mick nodded. "I'll consult with the museum staff, and see what I can find out. What about those names Madame Natasha came up with?"

Mom snorted. Bruce winced.

"I don't think we can trust anything she said," Maggie said.

Tania bit her lip. "But maybe they are real!"

Everyone looked at her. She turned to Mick. "I mean, you said they were reasonable French names. And that other stuff she said, that wasn't part of a name—where did she get that?" She looked around at everyone. "I know most of what she said was totally crazy. But who knows, maybe she got that part right."

She took a deep breath. I could see her steeling herself for what came next. "And remember the last two shows. She seemed to be doing something. Maybe she has some little gift, and it's just not as big as she pretends."

I grinned. It must've hurt, giving the Madame credit for even that much. But what else was she going to do?

The names were good clues, and how else could we convince anyone to take them seriously?

"I don't know," Mom said. "I think she was faking things all along."

"But what about the steamboat pilot?" Bruce said. "Something did happen that night, and she seemed to know about it."

Maggie was gazing at Tania. "Something did happen that night," she repeated. "I think Tania has a point. We can't assume the names are real, but we can look into them. See if there's any record of such people." She shrugged. "Who knows, maybe Madame Natasha actually did some research yesterday and found a real clue."

Mick nodded. "The names will give me someplace to start. There are some great research libraries in this city." He looked at Maggie, then down at his feet. "I could use some help."

"Sure," she said. "Just tell me what you want me to do."

He grinned at her. I wanted to step over there and punch him in the nose. But I figured it didn't matter how he felt about Maggie. She had more sense than to go for anyone like him.

Maggie glanced around and said softly, "We'd better start by working on the museum staff. Convince them we're not just a bunch of nuts, and they should still work with us."

Bruce nodded. "We'll do that right now. You'd better help me."

"Mick too," Maggie said. "He can prove that we know something about the French Renaissance, and are taking the research part seriously."

"Good. Annette?" Bruce looked at Mom.

"I'd better take care of the kids. But I have my cell phone if you need me for anything."

"All right." Bruce rubbed his hands together. "The rest of you are free to do as you like. We'll meet—when? The day after tomorrow? Does that give us time to find some answers?"

Maggie and Mick nodded.

"Good. Annette, maybe see if you can get a meeting room at the hotel. Nine a.m., day after tomorrow. I want everyone there, and we'll see what we have." He paused, and then muttered, "I sure hope we get something out of this."

"I'll take care of extending the hotel rooms," Mom said. "Except for Madame Natasha's," she added under her breath. "I'm taking her off the bill as soon as we get back there." She turned toward the exit. "Come on, kids."

"Can't we help somehow?" Tania asked.

"Leave the research to the experts," I said. I didn't want to spend the next day trapped in a library. Mick could make himself useful for once. As we trailed after Mom, I added softly, "We got things moving. Isn't that enough?"

Tania pouted as we wove through the museum and headed down the big staircase. "Anyway," I whispered to her, "we have more important things to do. Let them figure out who the squire was. We still have to figure out how to help him."

She nodded, and got that look of concentration. That should distract her for a little while. Until she came up with some crazy, impossible plan. Something sure to get results—and to get me in trouble.

CHAPTER
16

Two mornings later we headed for the meeting room at the hotel. Lionel slouched in a chair sipping the foam off a coffee drink. He wiggled his fingers in a wave.

Maggie held out a box of doughnuts. She's the best. "So what did you tourists do yesterday," she asked, "while some of us were working?"

"We took the ferry to the Statue of Liberty," I said, trying to sound casual about it.

"And Ellis Island!" Tania bounced on her toes. "It was neat! All those immigrants went through there, thousands of them. I wonder if any of our ancestors came through Ellis Island."

Maggie glanced at Lionel and raised her eyebrows. "Kids who like museums. They're getting awfully sophisticated."

I wasn't sure if that was a compliment or if she was

just teasing, so I grinned and didn't say anything.

Finally everyone gathered. We settled around the table, and Bruce stood up like this was some company board meeting. "All right, it's time to look at what we have, and see if we can turn this into a great *Haunted* show, or if we need to cut our losses and go home before we lose any more money. Who wants to report first?"

Mick looked at Maggie. "You tell it," he mumbled. Thank goodness. She'd be easier to listen to.

Maggie leaned back in her chair and smiled. "Well, much to our surprise, there actually was a knight named Alain Gulden. He lived near Paris and died in battle in 1569, at the age of thirty-two."

Everyone murmured in excitement. "The person who donated the sword to the museum wants to remain anonymous," Maggie added. "But according to the museum, the donor claimed that his grandfather bought the sword in Paris in the late 1800s. The sword has been dated to the sixteenth century."

"What about Hector Dubar?" Tania asked.

"That's a little trickier," Maggie said. "By a curious coincidence, we also have a record of someone by that name who died in the same battle. But who he was, we don't know. He wasn't listed as a knight, so he could have been a squire. Or he could have been something else entirely—a servant, a camp follower, maybe a priest. Who knows? We didn't find any more information about him. But it comes down to this: Either Madame Natasha already did some of this research before the séance, or somehow, by some miracle, she was telling the truth."

"She didn't go to that library," Mick said. "We asked."

"What about in disguise?" Lionel asked. It figures that a makeup artist would think of that.

Maggie shrugged. "That's harder to say. You have to show ID to use some of the resources, but does anybody know Madame Natasha's real name?"

She looked around. Everyone shook their heads.

"And it would be simple to disguise her," Lionel said. "I bet when you asked, you described a woman with flaming red hair and too much makeup. Take away the makeup, put her in jeans, pull her hair back in a bun, maybe under a hat or scarf—"

"All right, all right," Maggie said, "you've made your point. We don't know if Madame Natasha was there or not. She also might have found the information some-where else. But we do know that there was a knight named Alain Gulden, and a man named Hector Dubar who lived at the same time. Both of them died in the same battle. Right era, right place."

"We can use that," Bruce said. "Definitely!"

Maggie nodded. "We just have to be careful. Not claim that we found the real squire or anything, but present it as one possible option, a theory. The History Channel does things like that all the time."

Bruce said, "So the question is, how to turn all this into the perfect show? It's interesting, but we need something we can film. Something with people."

"We could ask the donor if the sword has a history of strange activity," Mom said.

Maggie shook her head. "The museum won't give out his name. They are willing to pass along a message, but if he wants to remain anonymous, he probably won't go on TV."

"And we're done with psychics," Bruce muttered.

Tania leaned forward. "Well, I actually did a little research at Ellis Island yesterday: I got on one of their computers. And I searched for the name 'Gulden.'"

Everyone was looking at her. "But honey," Mom said, "Ellis Island was only active in the late eighteen hundreds and early nineteen hundreds. And anyway, if Alain Gulden died in France, he certainly never emigrated here."

"I know, but I was just curious. Anyway, I found a man named Evrard Gulden who immigrated to the U.S. in 1895. He was twenty-nine years old, and came from France. He was the only Gulden listed."

"You think he might have been a descendant of Alain?" Maggie asked.

Tania nodded, bouncing in her seat. "Isn't it possible?"

Bruce put a hand to his chin. "A descendant . . . It's an idea. If we can find one, we can interview him about family history, see if there are any legends." He looked at Mick. "Can you look into it?"

"Sure, you can get a lot of records online these days. I can hook up to the Internet here." He leaned forward, opened his laptop, and started typing.

People chatted. I leaned toward Tania. "Just what do you hope to accomplish with this?"

"The ghost wants to give the sword back to Alain Gulden," she whispered. "But he's dead. So how about one of his descendants? Isn't that the closest thing?"

"I guess so. If you can make him understand it all."

"There has to be some way we can make it work! I picked up a French phrasebook when we stopped in that big bookstore. Now we can talk to Hector Dubar ourselves."

"Won't that be fun," I said. "So all we have to do is find a descendant, get back to the museum again, and make sure the ghost knows what's happening, speaking French out of a book. And we can't let anyone else know."

106

CHAPTER
17

All right, I found a few Guldens in the greater New York area," Mick said "Not as many as you would think; it's an unusual name, I guess. Some don't have an address or phone number. But here's one woman, Marcia, who lives in Brooklyn."

Maggie leaned over to look at his computer. "I'll try calling her." She pulled out her cell phone and dialed.

Someone answered, and after a brief greeting, Maggie explained that we were doing some genealogical research on the Guldens. She didn't mention ghosts. She listened for a bit, thanked the woman and hung up. "No good. Gulden is her married name. Her husband died ten years ago. She doesn't really know anything about the family."

She and Mick studied the computer and made a few more calls. Other people chatted, tossing out ideas.

Maggie snapped her phone shut. "Another answering machine. One disconnected number, one no answer. And one who barely spoke English, but I did get that he was Norwegian, not French."

"Here's a Marc Gulden who has his bio online," Mick said. "He's an actor. And it says he speaks French. That's a good sign, right?"

"And an actor," Bruce murmured. "That means he'll be presentable on film."

Lionel hopped up and leaned over Mick's shoulder to peer at the computer screen. "He's in an off-Broadway play right now. Actually, off-off-Broadway."

"What does that mean?" Tania asked.

"Broadway is the real thing, the big deal, the main stage where everyone wants to perform," Lionel said. "In the more literal sense, it's also a large street with lots of theaters and neon lights. If you make it to Broadway, you've made it as a performer. The smaller theaters are off-Broadway. And the really small theaters, where they try out new plays by unknown playwrights, are off-off-Broadway. Tourists hardly ever go to those theaters, only locals."

"In other words, this guy isn't very good," I said.

"Hey, you have to start somewhere," Lionel said. "Maybe we're just meeting him before he's famous. Anyway, it looks like he's in an improv troupe. Improvisation is hard, making things up on the spot. "

"Is there a number for the actor?" Maggie asked.

Mick read it out to her and she dialed. Maggie introduced herself and they talked for a few minutes. She put her hand over the mouthpiece. "He says his great grandfather immigrated from France. Family legend has it that they were minor nobility in the Middle Ages. It's not proof, but it's something."

Bruce nodded. "Let's set up an interview."

Maggie smiled and spoke into the phone. "How would you like to be interviewed for our TV show?"

They started making plans. Finally she snapped the phone closed and smiled around at everyone. "He's available this afternoon! I told him I'd call back when I knew where we wanted to do the interview."

"Oh, but you have to do it at the museum!" Tania said. "It would be really interesting if you filmed at the museum, with the sword. Mr. Gulden could talk about how this would have been his ancestor's sword. Maybe the museum will even let him hold it."

"We might not be able to get in on such short notice," Mom said. "They have a lot of paperwork."

"We can find one of these old stone buildings, with the Gothic architecture," Maggie said. "Use that as a background."

Tania looked at me and bit her lip. I said, "But won't

it seem kind of funny if this guy's ancestor owned the sword, and we don't even have the sword in the shot?"

"Well . . ." Bruce frowned. "The museum would be nice."

"You could charm them," Tania said, "so they'll be willing to let us shoot there today."

Bruce smiled. "Thanks for the vote of confidence. I guess we can try."

"I'll call for a meeting right now," Mom said. "I'll point out that TV exposure will draw the tourists. They'll like that, whether they believe in the ghost or not!"

"Great!" Tania said. "We'll come along. While you're talking with people, Jon and I can look around the museum some more."

Mom chuckled. "I'm delighted that you're getting so excited about art. But I don't really want you two wandering around by yourself."

"But Mom, we'll be inside the museum, and we'll be together. It's perfectly safe."

"Even so," Mom said, "I'd rather you had someone with you."

She glanced around. I looked at Maggie, hoping she'd volunteer. But Tania said, "How about Mick? Mick, would you join us?"

Mick looked at her and then at me. I tried to smile at him.

"Sure, okay, I guess." He looked at Mom, and kind of cringed. "If it's all right with you, Annette."

Mom stared at him for a second, and then at Tania and me. "Well, all right, if you really want to. Thank you, Mick, that's very kind of you."

Mick smiled and relaxed. Mom and Bruce needed to set up appointments, so Tania and I got in a cab with Mick. Tania chatted on the way up, trying to keep him charmed. Mick actually laughed a couple of times. I didn't know he knew how.

As we went up the museum steps, Tania pulled out her phrasebook. "Oh, Mick, I'm trying to learn French. I want to be able to do what you do, the way you talked to that ghost."

Mick puffed his chest out and smiled. Yeah, big hero.

"You can help me." For a second I thought Tania was actually going to bat her eyelashes at him. "As we go through the museum, you can help me practice."

"Sure," Mick said. "What do you want to see today?"

"Oh, we can wander all over," Tania said. She added casually, "And I wouldn't mind going back to the armor room, maybe taking another look at that sword. We might get some ideas that will help the show."

We headed into the museum. Tania obviously had

Mick wrapped around her little finger. I hoped she could keep him there. Maybe he was acting nicer, but I still didn't trust him. And he'd have to be even dumber than he acted not to get some idea of what was going on. If he figured out that Tania could see ghosts, I had no idea what he would do.

I hoped I didn't have to find out.

CHAPTER
18

I tried to take an interest in the stuff we saw as we wandered the museum, to throw Mick off the scent. But of course, Tania and I were really thinking about the ghost. We managed to get there in about half an hour, without making it obvious that we were anxious.

"So," Tania said, as we wandered through the room with the mounted armor, "say they find this descendant of the ghost knight. And they want to do an interview here, and maybe tell the ghost that they have the knight's descendant. How would you say that in French?"

Mick chuckled. "You know, most people start with the basics. Hello, how are you, where's the bathroom, that kind of thing. That's a lot more practical."

Tania smiled at him. "Maybe for most people, but we're ghost investigators. This is the kind of French you've been using, right?"

"I guess so."

Tania had been strolling toward the sword room, and now had Mick in the doorway. I saw her eyes flick to the corner of the room, and she smiled as if greeting someone. "So, let's see. We would want to say, Hector Dubar, we want to help you."

Mick said it in French, and Tania repeated it after him. "And then we want to say, the knight you served has perished in battle."

"Uh . . . does it have to be perished? Can I just say he died?"

"Well, if you have to. But I figured maybe the ghost would be sensitive about that. We don't want to upset him."

Mick smiled. "A sensitive ghost, sure." He came up with something in French. Tania copied it, and then had him say, "We found a descendant of the knight." We weren't sure that was true, but Tania had flexible ideas about truth sometimes.

All this time, Tania was glancing between Mick and the corner of the room. Maybe she thought she was being subtle, but it looked funny. Like she was looking at something that wasn't there. Mick watched her closely. He'd soon realize something was going on. But I couldn't think of how to signal Tania, or distract Mick, without doing something just as obvious.

Tania hesitated a moment, her eyes moving as if

watching something come closer. Finally she said, "And then I guess we want to ask him if that's all right. Would you give up the sword to a descendant. Would that fulfill your duty, so you can move on."

Mick glanced to where she'd been looking, and said something in French. Tania repeated it softly, while Mick watched her, and then she smiled.

"Okay!" I said. "That was a great French lesson. Should we move on to something else now?"

Tania turned with a grin. "Sure. That was great, Mick, thanks."

"No problem. And here's a more useful phrase for you." He said something else in French. "That means, 'I'm going to go find a bathroom.' Practical French. Why don't you two wait for me right here."

We agreed and he left the room. Tania grinned at me and clapped her hands. "We did it! It's going to work!"

"What exactly happened?"

"Oh, it was perfect. The squire understood everything. When I said that the knight had died, he made the sign of the cross. He seemed kind of sad, but not really surprised. Do you think he's known all this time, that he's protecting the sword for a dead man?"

"Could be. Maybe he figured it out when a few hundred years passed and he didn't see his boss. Or maybe it was when they brought the sword here to the museum. He has to realize this isn't the world he knew. Anyway, he said it was all right? He'd give the sword to a descendant?"

"Yes. I had to guess at what he was actually saying, of course, since I couldn't ask Mick to translate. But when I said we found a descendant, he got excited. He asked something, but I don't know what. And then when I said could he give the sword to the descendant, he bowed, very serious. So I'm sure it's all right."

"Great. I hope this actor really is a descendant."

"The ghost won't know otherwise." Tania bounced. "Mick isn't so bad, is he? He's been a big help."

"Yeah, I guess so. Though I think he just wants to get in good with Mom."

I turned and stepped out of the room and found myself face-to-face with Mick.

CHAPTER
19

Mick!" I gasped.

He stared at me, his eyes wide and mouth half open. How much had he heard? He couldn't have left the room more than two or three minutes before. It had to have taken him that long to get to the bathroom and back. But the look on his face showed he'd heard *something*.

My mind scrambled back. At the end, we'd been talking about him—whether he was nice or not. Hopefully that was what got him worked up.

"Um, look, Mick, about what I was just saying . . . about Mom, I mean, it's okay. You're being nice now, so that's cool."

He kept staring at me, but I'm not sure he even saw me. His gaze slid over to Tania. "It's true," he whispered.

We both froze.

"They are real," he said. "Ghosts are real! And you—you can actually see this one?"

Tania was pale. I tried to laugh. "Oh, Mick, you didn't take that seriously, did you? We were just joking around. You must have misheard and . . ."

He was still staring at Tania. She gazed back, pleading with her big blue eyes, not saying anything. Where were her lies now?

"Please tell me, please," he said softly, "are ghosts real?"

Tania took a deep breath and let it out slowly, her eyes still locked on Mick's. "You have to keep it a secret."

"It's all right," he said. "I won't tell anyone."

"Yes, they're real."

He broke into a grin. "I knew it! I grew up in this old house, and I used to hear voices. My parents always said it was just wind coming through the cracks. But sometimes I heard laughter. I'd swear it was laughter, and I just knew, I knew it was ghosts. But then when I got older, I thought it couldn't be, and now . . ." He paused his rambling for a moment, then said solemnly, "It's true. They are real. You can see them, actually see them?"

Tania nodded. He turned to me. "And you?"

I shook my head. He lost interest in me and looked back at Tania. It made me angry all over again that I couldn't see them. Not because I wanted Mick to be impressed, but why was Tania special, and I wasn't? I tried to help the ghosts too. Why didn't I get to see them?

"Why don't you want people to know?" he asked.

"It's really just a bunch of little things," Tania said. "Bruce would want to put me on the show, and lots of people would think I was crazy, or lying. And we had a sister who died a couple of years ago. Mom got into all this ghost stuff because she wanted to contact Angela. She never said so, but that's what we figure. So she'd want me to do that. But ghosts don't work that way."

"I didn't know Annette lost a child. So that's why she's always fussing about you. I just thought she was controlling, like my parents."

People came into the big room. I nudged Tania back into the sword room. "Come on guys, if we're going to talk about this, let's keep it down."

Mick looked all around, as if he might see the ghost this time. "So where is he? What does he look like?"

Tania described the ghost, in a lot more detail than when I had asked. Like, he had on a green tunic and brown hose. Mick even wanted to know what kind of boots he had.

"Can you talk to him?" Mick asked.

"I can hear him, but I can't understand what he's saying."

Mick nodded rapidly. "That's why you needed me, and the French. I knew something was up. Sorry for spying on you, but I just had to know. Now we can interview him together!"

He was grinning like an idiot, and Tania returned the look. "If you ask the questions, I can tell you what he says. It's been so hard not knowing."

"This is great!" Mick waved his arms. "No one else has this opportunity to actually interview someone from the sixteenth century. We can get all kinds of details about his life. I could write a paper about it, go back to college and make it my thesis. We should get a tape recorder, record the interviews."

"Hey, wait a minute," I said. "We're trying to keep this a secret, and help the ghost. I don't think we'll have time for a research project." I glared at Mick. "It's a secret, get it? We can't do anything that would make Mom suspicious."

"I won't." Mick stared at me for a minute. "I heard what else you said, about me trying to get in good with your mom. I know Annette doesn't like me."

Tania kind of laughed. "Oh, don't be silly, Mick. Of course Mom likes you."

He shook his head. "I'm not good at telling how people feel, but it's pretty obvious she can't stand me."

"It's not that she doesn't like you," Tania said. "It's

just that she, maybe . . ." She trailed off and looked at me. I couldn't think of anything to say. After all, I was pretty sure he was right.

"People don't like me," Mick muttered. "I try to do a good job. I work hard. I finish most of my research before we go on the shoots, so I try to make myself useful in other ways. I'm always looking for extra things that need to be done. Crowd control, stuff like that."

"I haven't heard anyone complain about your work," Tania said.

"It's more, like, you're not always nice," I said. I couldn't believe where this conversation was going.

"But I try to be nice!" Mick said. "I help out whenever I can. I don't know what I do wrong." He looked at me. "See, you said I hate you. People always think I don't like them, or I'm mean to them or something. But I'm not trying to be mean."

I gaped at him. "Do you remember on the steamboat, when you got me in trouble?"

He looked at his feet and shrugged. "Well, yeah, but you were messing around with that wrench. I was just trying to help out. I was trying to look after things, watch for trouble, you know."

Okay, he had a point. I had been doing something wrong, sort of. But, still.

"Look, Mick," Tania said, "I'm sure you're a nice

guy. Maybe you just have to try harder to show people how nice you can be."

"But how do I do that?"

I said, "Don't try to get people in trouble."

"Right," Tania agreed. "Try assuming the best about people, instead of the worst."

"Ask questions before you make accusations," I said.

"And maybe don't worry so much about working hard," Tania added. "Just do your job, and let other people do theirs. If Mom wants you to do something extra, like crowd control, she'll ask."

Mick looked at her, then me, his eyes as hopeful as a puppy begging for scraps. "You really think that will work?"

I shrugged. "It couldn't make things worse."

Tania beamed at him. "I'm sure it will make a difference! We'll help you, right Jon?"

I managed not to groan. "Sure."

"That's great!" Mick was grinning. "And we'll get to work together, on the ghosts."

"Yeah, but about that—" I said.

I paused at the sound of voices. A blond kid of about five or six ran into the room, followed by a tired-looking Hispanic woman with a baby in a stroller.

The kid ran up to the glass case and pressed his face

against it. "Sword! Sword! I want it." He started pounding his fists on the case.

Tania glanced at the kid, and then at something next to him. "Oh, wait—stop!" I wasn't sure if she was talking to the kid, or to the ghost. She reached out a hand, about a foot to the left of the kid.

She gasped and pulled her hand back. "He's upsetting him!" she hissed to Mick. "Tell him it's all right. The boy can't hurt the sword."

The tired woman looked at us and said something in Spanish. I moved to block her view. "It's all right, we're just, um . . . they're just . . ."

I heard shuffling sounds behind me. Mick said, "Be careful, son, stand back."

I glanced over my shoulder. Mick was leaning forward to take the kid's arms. The woman pushed past me and grabbed at Mick, yelling something. Worry and frustration built up around us, along with an icy cold.

"Tania, get out of here," I said.

Mick said something to the woman in Spanish. The little boy turned around and kicked him in the shin.

Mick staggered backward, to where the ghost must have been.

Tania screamed. "Look out!"

Mick froze for a second, eyes wide. He shuddered from head to foot. Then he staggered forward, grabbed the boy and kind of tossed him out of the room, shoving the woman after.

Mick knocked against my shoulder and stumbled back. His arms flailed as he tried to get his balance again. Tania and I pressed back against the wall.

Mick must have stumbled into the ghost again. A blast of cold filled the room.

It lifted Mick right off his feet and slammed him into the wall.

CHAPTER

20

Mick slumped to the floor. The woman's jabbering voice faded into the distance. Was she going for help, reporting us to the security guard, or just getting away from the insanity?

Tania and I stared at Mick. He didn't move. I was pretty sure the loud thunk I'd heard was his head hitting the wall.

"Mick?" Tania whispered.

I forced myself to breathe. "What's the ghost doing now?"

"He went forward and looked down at Mick, and then he backed away. I didn't understand what he said, but I think he was apologizing. Anyway, he's back in the corner. I don't think he's going to do anything else."

"Okay." I took a couple of steps forward, trying to remember my first aid from the Scouts. Don't move him, that was the most important thing. I touched his shoulder lightly. "Mick? Can you hear me?"

He groaned and moved a little on his own. I let out my breath, my legs suddenly weak with relief. "Come on, Mick. Are you all right? Do we need to call an ambulance?" I really didn't want to do that. All those questions. And how would Mom feel, if the guy who was supposed to be looking after us got taken to the hospital?

Mick's eyelids fluttered, and finally opened. He moaned again. He started to sit up, so I helped him.

Tania crouched beside us. "Mick, are you all right?"

He blinked a few times. "Oh, it's you two." His voice sounded thick. "My head." He put a hand to his forehead. "What happened?"

Tania opened her mouth, but I glanced at her and shook my head quickly. "What do you remember?" I asked.

Mick rubbed his forehead. "We were looking at the sword and talking about . . . French costumes? I can't quite remember. Something about the ghost." He frowned in concentration. I held my breath. Finally Mick shrugged, and kind of half laughed. "It's stupid. Somehow I have this idea that we saw the ghost."

"Saw it?" Tania asked.

"Yeah, something like that. I know it's impossible. And I can't even really picture it now, it's just a vague impression. But it's like I was really excited that the ghost was real." He shook his head, then groaned. "That must've been quite a bump. My memory is all messed up. I guess maybe I was unconscious for a minute, and had some dreams. I couldn't have really seen a ghost." He looked around the room, as if double-checking.

"There's nothing to see," I said.

Mick sighed. "Yeah. Just wishful thinking."

"Do you need a doctor?" Tania asked.

He shook his head, then winced and put his hand up to it. "No, I think I'll be all right. But maybe we should go sit down for a while. What did I do, anyway?"

Someone filled the doorway. "Everything all right in here?"

We looked up at the guard. "He tripped and bumped his head against the wall," I said. "But it's all right."

The guard wanted Mick to fill out an accident report, but we managed to get away without giving our names. Mick stopped in the bathroom to splash cold water on his face. Tania and I waited outside. "Has he really forgotten?" she asked.

I shrugged. "Maybe it will come back to him. I've heard of temporary amnesia."

"Shouldn't we tell him? He was so excited."

"Yeah, but a little too excited. Talking about recording interviews and writing a paper. Tania, your goal is to help this ghost move on, right?"

127

She nodded.

"Well, Mick will want him to stick around, to be researched. That's not helping the ghost, it's helping Mick. And do you really think we can keep this a secret if Mick is running around with you and a tape recorder? The fewer people who know, the better."

She sighed. "You're right. But it's too bad. I was starting to like him. And he was useful."

"Yeah, but you've done what you came to do. The ghost will be ready if we get that descendant in here. Better leave it at that."

The crew got permission to film at the museum again, after hours, that evening. For dinner, we went to this haunted house kind of place, where they had torture devices and monster masks on the wall. Actors put on a horror skit. It was fun, but kind of weird because everything was fake, when we'd just been with a real ghost. Of course, I couldn't see the real ghost, and I could see the fake stuff.

Afterward, we headed back to the museum once again. It was almost starting to feel like home. The actor, Marc, was waiting in the lobby when the guard let us in. He bounded over and shook hands with everyone.

"My first chance at TV!" he said. "Some of the stage actors will think I'm selling out, but I can hardly wait." He was probably in his thirties, with brown hair and a thin face. You wouldn't have noticed him on the street.

We hauled all the equipment back to the Arms and Armor department. They had moved a fancy, old-looking table into the big room. The sword lay on it, on a soft white cloth. One of the museum employees gave Bruce a look. "We didn't have any trouble moving it when you weren't here."

Another employee said, "Well, it did get cold."

The first man shrugged. "I still say it's just a glitch in the air conditioning."

Bruce just smiled. "We really appreciate you letting us film again. The museum has been so wonderful."

The employee sniffed. "They seem to think it's worth the publicity. We want the National Museum to be accessible and enjoyable to all kinds of people."

"I'm sure the show will create a lot of interest," Bruce said. "It's good for all of us." It was interesting to watch him turn on the charm, and see it actually work.

It took a while to get the cameras set up. I watched the actor while Lionel gave him TV makeup. Marc didn't look like anyone special when his face was still. But when Lionel finished, and Marc started chatting, his whole face lit up. I guess that's what they mean by an animated face.

Tania was reviewing her French phrasebook, quietly mumbling things.

"Where's the ghost now?" I asked.

"He's in the doorway of the sword room. Maybe he's gotten used to being in there, and feels safer or something. Come on." She edged toward it.

Tania said something in French. I recognized the word for "knight," since I'd been hearing it. Another word sounded kind of like "descendant."

She frowned at the empty air, bit her lip, and flipped through the book.

Mom said, "All right, places everyone. Kids, move back, please."

Tania muttered her French phrase again, and then we backed across the room. "What's up?" I asked.

"I'm not sure. I told him that this was a descendant who was going to take possession of the sword. But I can't figure out what he said. This darn phrasebook, it's so hard to look up words when you only hear the French."

"Uh-oh. Don't forget, this guy is, like, four hundred years old. He probably speaks old-fashioned, like Shakespeare."

They started filming. Bruce asked Marc Gulden about his family history. He talked about his great-grandfather immigrating, and the family stories.

"What's the ghost doing?" I whispered to Tania.

"Walking back and forth. He doesn't look happy. He's muttering something, but I can't catch it from here."

I started to get a bad feeling. I guess I wasn't the only one. The skeptical museum employee started pacing, and muttering, "I don't like this. This isn't a good idea."

Mom was watching the filming. She shook her head. "Something's not quite right."

Tania flipped through her phrasebook. "*Anglais, Anglais*. That means English. He thinks Marc Gulden is English! I guess he hears Marc speaking English and doesn't see how he could be related to a French knight."

"You want try explaining immigration to him?" I asked.

"Oh, what are we going to do?" Tania wailed.

"Stand back," I said. "It's about to get worse."

CHAPTER
21

"How do you know?"

"The ghost is getting emotional, right?" I asked.

"Yes, he keeps pacing, and now he's shaking his fist at Marc."

Bruce said, "So, Mr. Gulden, your ancestor, the *cochon*—wait, sorry, what did I just say?"

Marc was staring at him. "*Cochon*—that's French for 'pig.' Are you trying to suggest something?"

Bruce shook his head. "I don't know where that came from. I didn't even know what it meant. I guess I just tripped over my own tongue." Bruce fiddled with his tie. "Stephan, stop filming for a minute."

"*Cochon*, that's what Hector Dubar has been calling Marc!" Tania said. "*Cochon Anglais*—an English pig."

"And Bruce somehow picked up on it? Whoa." I imagined the short French squire pacing around, waving his fists and calling a twenty-first-century New York actor an English pig. I couldn't help it; I started to laugh.

"Quiet!" Mick snapped. So much for being nice. Then he put a hand to his forehead and moaned, and I felt a little bad.

"What do you think, Maggie?" Mom asked. "Somehow this isn't going quite right. I'm not sure what's missing, but . . ."

Maggie nodded and rubbed her arms. "Maybe it's just because it's getting cold in here again, but you're right, something feels off."

"It's my first time on TV," Marc was saying. "Give me another chance, I'll get it right."

Lionel put a hand on his shoulder. "You've been doing great." He turned his back on Bruce and whispered, "But Bruce's questions could use some work."

"I can try moving the camera," Stephan said, "but this room is just so boring. We shouldn't be shooting against that wall. We should turn so we have the mounted armor in the background."

"That's stupid," the other cameraman said. "It will look too cluttered."

Voices tumbled over one another. They were all talking about different things, but they all seemed to agree: Something was wrong.

Mom clapped her hands. "Listen, everyone! Let's

133

take a little break. In fifteen minutes, we'll start over."

People grumbled. They spread out in the room, still arguing in small groups.

"You'd better calm down your ghost," I told Tania. "He's getting everyone worked up."

She nodded and scurried forward, still clutching the phrasebook. I followed and tried to stand where it would look like she was talking to me, but not where the ghost was.

She hissed something, choppy words that obviously weren't complete sentences. Then she stamped her foot. "Oh, I wish I could make him understand! He keeps calling Marc an English pig, and from his gestures I think he just said that he'll kill Marc if he touches the sword."

"Yikes. I wonder if he actually could. We better come up with a plan B quickly, so we don't have to find out."

"But what? How can we convince Hector Dubar that Marc Gulden is actually a descendent of the knight?"

I looked across the room, to where the actor was talking with Lionel. Marc didn't particularly look French to me, and he sure didn't sound it. He was supposed to know French, but even if we got him to speak in French, he just looked so modern. It probably wasn't what the squire was expecting in a descendant.

"He'll want somebody dressed old-fashioned," I

said, "and speaking French. We need to get him in costume."

"Right," Tania said. "Let's talk to Mom and see what we can do."

Mom was huddled with Bruce and Maggie. "I just knew this wasn't going to work," Bruce said. "This whole episode is cursed!"

"Now stop it," Mom said. "Just because you investigate ghosts doesn't mean you have to get all superstitious. We've had some bad luck, but we can work it out."

"The interview wasn't even bad," Maggie said. "It just felt kind of . . ."

"Boring," I said. They turned to look at Tania and me.

"This whole descendant interview was your idea," Bruce grumbled.

"Okay, but it needs something else. If you want to make this a great show, you need to be creative."

Maggie smiled. "And just what do you suggest?"

"Well, remember at the haunted hotel, how you had an actress dress up as the ghost?"

"You think we should do that?" Mom asked. "Have someone act like the ghost, and maybe have Marc Gulden talk to him?"

I shook my head. "No, I think you should do it the

other way around. You should have Marc dressed in Renaissance clothes, like he was the knight."

"Like his ancestor!" Tania said.

"Not bad," Bruce said. "But then what? I just interview Marc while he's dressed up?"

"His bio says that he speaks French, right? So have him speak French." I was thinking fast. "Maybe someone else could dress up as the squire, and give the sword to him." That would get the sword "returned," if we could get the ghost to go along with it.

"Or Marc could give the sword to someone else," Maggie said. "If he's the descendant of the knight, then we can re-create the scene where the knight gives the sword to the squire, telling him to keep it safe."

"That could work," Mom said. "But we have to get the costumes."

"Let's talk to Marc about it," Bruce said.

They turned and headed for Marc and Lionel. I looked at Tania and shrugged. "It's something, anyway."

"Yeah. At least it gets Marc dressed as a French knight, and holding the sword. We just have to convince Hector Dubar that he's fulfilled his duty and can move on, before Marc passes the sword off to someone else."

We went to where the group was now talking in excited voices. "The costume is no problem," Marc said.

"I know where I can get that tomorrow morning. And I'm free all day, there's no show tomorrow."

Tania grinned at me. "It's all working out."

Mom clapped her hands. "Oh, and I have a wonderful idea! We've done so much shooting in this museum. It is getting a little dull, being back in the same room. But I was talking to the museum's publicity person earlier today, about the National Museum's other branch. And I think we can work this out. Tomorrow, instead of shooting here, we can do the re-creation at The Monastery!"

Tania and I exchanged panicked looks. "What? Wait, Mom, where's this place?" I asked.

"Mom, what's wrong with the museum?" Tania said. "It's nice here."

Mom shook her head. "No, Jon was right when he said it was boring. And The Monastery is just wonderful. It's up on the north point of Manhattan."

"It was actually built from pieces of real monasteries, right?" Maggie said.

Mom nodded. "That they brought over from France! It's a beautiful setting, all the stone walls and arched windows. It's French, it's from about the right time— the re-creation will look real."

Bruce gave her a hug. "Brilliant!"

They were off and running. Tania and I made a few

more stabs at trying to persuade them to stay at the museum. It didn't do any good.

We pulled back from the group. "It probably doesn't matter," I said. "The plan should work there just as well."

"But how will Hector Dubar get there?"

"He'll follow the sword, right? That must be how he got here."

"Maybe, but what if something goes wrong? What if he's tired himself out so much these last few days that he can't travel with the sword? Or even if he does, he could get upset and cause trouble when they try to move it. And when he gets there, he'll see Marc getting into costume and figure out what's going on."

I had to admit, there were a lot of things that could screw up. "I don't see what we can do about it."

Tania was staring into space with a frown of concentration. "We have to keep track of the squire, keep control. We have to know where he is and what he's doing." She met my eyes. "I've been possessed by ghosts before."

"Wait a minute—"

"It makes sense," she said. "The best way to keep track of Hector Dubar is if his spirit is inside of me."

CHAPTER
22

didn't sleep much that night. I couldn't decide what to do about Tania and the ghost. Helping the squire was important to her. I hadn't always been admitting it, but it was important to me too. Maybe ghosts didn't feel as real to me, since I couldn't see them. But if I let myself think about it, I could imagine being the squire. Trapped in a weird world. Always on the alert as hundreds of strangers poured through his room every day. Never able to rest, except maybe at night when the museum was dark and empty and lonely. Thinking, always, about his failure, and not knowing how to make it better.

But did Tania really have to let the ghost possess her in order to help him?

When I brought it up again in the morning, she said, "This will be our last chance. We can't risk anything going wrong. They're going to take the sword up to The Monastery in a car. Can you imagine Hector Dubar traveling through New York City crammed in a car with the museum staff? He could get upset, cause a wreck, hurt people." She shook her head. "We have to do it my way, if we can. I'll be able to control him."

But could she?

"Okay, but . . ." I couldn't believe I was actually going to say this. "I think we need to ask Mick for help."

"*You* want to tell Mick?"

"No! I hate the idea that he found out anything, and I'd like him to just forget all about it. But this is too much for us alone."

I took a deep breath. "It's not like with the ghost bride, where we only had to get you ten minutes to the cemetery—and that was hard enough. And it's not like the phantom pilot, where we were right there on the boat the whole time, and which still scared me half to death, by the way. We have to get from one museum to the other, across the city, with Mom and all kinds of other people around. I'll need help."

Tania smiled. "I think that's the first time I've heard you say that. I'll call Mick's room."

She dialed, listened, and hung up. "No answer. He's probably already down at breakfast."

We headed for the hotel dining room. For once, I

didn't have much of an appetite. My stomach was in knots. They actually loosened a little when I saw Mick at the buffet. He wasn't much of an ally, but I was desperate.

A cheery voice called out behind us. "Morning, sunshines!"

"Oh hi, Lionel," Tania said.

"You're keeping me company this morning, right honey? How about over there?" He started for a table.

Tania whispered, "I'll keep him busy. You talk to Mick."

I walked up to Mick in the buffet line. "Hey, how's it going?"

"Oh, it's you." He scowled, and I remembered all the times he'd been a pain.

"Yeah . . . so how's your head?"

"I hardly got any sleep," he grumbled. "It still hurts. And I have this big lump, thanks to you."

"*Me?*"

"Don't play innocent with me. Maybe I don't remember exactly what happened, but I know you were up to your tricks. You were trying to play a prank on me, or get rid of me or something. And look what happened!"

I stared at him. Mean Mick was back.

He slapped a couple of sausages on his plate and

shoved the tongs back in the tray. "I'm tired and my head hurts, so just stay away from me today. You got that?"

"Oh, I got it."

He lumbered off to the far corner of the room. I grabbed a plate and filled it, hardly looking at what I was getting. I felt kind of numb as I crossed the room and sat with Tania and Lionel. Tania perched on the edge of a chair, her body stiff and straight. Her eyes looked too big—scared, but determined. She looked at me, and I shook my head.

I stared down at my food. My throat felt so tight, I wasn't sure I could swallow.

"You both look a little pale," Lionel said. "Better have a nice breakfast."

"I'm not hungry," Tania said.

"Eat something," I grunted. "You'll need energy today." I picked at my pancakes.

Tania got a muffin and nibbled at it while Lionel talked. "It's great being in New York. I've managed to see a play every night. I just love the theater!"

"So why aren't you living here," I snapped, "instead of in Los Angeles?"

"I'm from California. I guess I never quite had the nerve to pack it all up and come to the Big Apple. I've been grateful for a steady job with *Haunted*, but . . ." He sighed. "My first love really is the stage. That energy, every night. The camaraderie between the performers. Their willingness to believe."

"Believe what?" Tania asked.

Lionel laughed. "Oh, anything! You've never met a more superstitious bunch. Maybe it's dressing up every night, pretending to be someone else. But in the theater, you can believe anything. You can believe in magic."

Tania's eyes were intensely focused on Lionel. "Can you believe in ghosts?"

Lionel grinned. "Darling, I can believe six impossible things before breakfast. Ghosts are easy! Most old theaters have one or two. When I was in high school, I volunteered at a community theater. We used to hear strange noises, and sometimes the lights would go out. It was an old building, and people claimed that back in the thirties a director fell from the catwalk and died. People said he was still haunting the theater, trying to give his advice on how to run a show."

"But you've never actually seen a ghost?" Tania asked.

Lionel shook his head. "More's the pity. Just think, if I could only see our museum ghost, I could practice my French."

Tania stared at him.

"I didn't realize I was that fascinating," Lionel said.

She said slowly, "If I tell you something, will you promise to keep it a secret?"

He put a hand on his chest. "Honey, I'm even better at keeping secrets than I am at believing the impossible."

She took a deep breath. I held mine, waiting. Was she really going to do what I thought she was going to do? I glanced around the restaurant, making sure no one else was listening.

"The thing is," Tania said, "we could use your help."

He made a motion like he was tipping an invisible hat. "Always happy to be of service."

"It's about the ghost." She explained.

CHAPTER
23

Lionel didn't laugh, or ask if we thought he was stupid and were playing a trick on him. He just listened, nodding once in a while. When Tania finished, he rubbed his hands together and grinned. "It's the best thing I've heard in years. Of course I'll help you."

Tania sighed and relaxed back into her chair. I started breathing normally again. I wasn't quite sure how I felt. On the one hand, it was nice to have another ally. A grown-up, who could do some things we couldn't. I wouldn't be the only one responsible for Tania, for making this work. And Lionel was nicer than Mick.

On the other hand, it wasn't just our secret anymore. How much would Lionel want to take over? Could he really be trusted?

We were about to find out. I glanced at my watch. "We're supposed to meet Mom and Bruce in ten minutes. Time to make this work."

First stop, the National Museum. Mom, Bruce, and Maggie headed for the offices to check in with the museum staff. Lionel said we'd meet them by the sword.

My heart was racing as we walked through the museum, and my palms felt sweaty. This was one of those days where you knew something major was going to happen. But you didn't know whether it was good or bad, and you couldn't control it.

By the time we got to the Medieval department, Tania was white and trembling. "Are you sure you want to do this?" I asked. Suddenly, anything else seemed easier. Smarter. Safer.

But she nodded, eyes on the sword room as we crossed to it. "This is what I was meant to do." I wasn't sure how to take that. It really was her crusade—but it seemed like too much for an eleven-year-old girl.

We stepped into the sword room. Tania took a deep breath and managed to smile at the thing I couldn't see. "*Bonjour*, Hector Dubar," she said.

"All right, Lionel," I said. "You're up."

He cleared his throat and started speaking in French. I have to admit, he didn't sound as good as Mick. He stumbled a bit, and hesitated in places. But if he was doing his job, he was explaining the situation to Hector Dubar. Or at least he was explaining what we wanted the squire to think.

Lionel finished and looked at Tania. She nodded and seemed to be listening. Then she said something slowly in French. For the first time in my life, I really wished I could understand a foreign language. Tania was frustrated because she could hear but not understand. Lionel could understand but not hear. But I couldn't hear *or* understand the ghost. I didn't like being dependent on other people.

"Whew!" Lionel brushed sweat from his forehead. "This accent, the old-fashioned language, is tough. But I think we got through to him. He's willing to go with us."

"Tell him that the sword will be out of his sight for a little while," Tania said.

Lionel spoke in French, and then Tania repeated what the ghost said. "He doesn't like it," Lionel said. "But he agrees. He said we're the first people to talk to him in many years. He's weary, and he wants to finish this. So he'll trust us."

Tania listened and added something else in French. Lionel gave a quick grin and winked at me. "Even if you do look English."

"Thanks a bunch," I muttered. "I think I hear people; we'd better hurry."

Tania took a deep breath and stepped forward. I clenched my fists, resisting the urge to go after her, to pull her back. I'd seen what happened when she'd gotten possessed before. It won't be like Rose, I told myself. Rose, the ghost bride we'd met on our first show, wasn't just dead, she was crazy. This time, it would be like the steamboat pilot. When he took over Tania's body, he was able to steer the boat, to save us from disaster. That time had been good. This had to be like that.

"How exactly does this work?" For the first time, Lionel sounded jittery.

I swallowed. "We're kind of making this up as we go along."

Tania reached out both hands. Her fingers curled around something invisible. She closed her eyes and trembled.

Lionel took a step forward. "Tania!"

I hesitated, not sure whether to go help, or tell him to keep back. What would happen if we interfered now?

Lionel grabbed Tania's arms from behind, but jerked back the moment he touched her. "She's cold!"

"Good," I croaked. "That means it's working."

Tania moaned and swayed. I carefully reached for her arm. My fingers went numb, but I held on. "Tania, you all right? Are you in there?"

She turned her face to me, but her eyes didn't focus. In a voice that was her voice, but not, she said something in French.

CHAPTER
24

Lionel pressed back against the wall. "Oh man, oh man, it's real!"

"You didn't believe us?" I asked.

"I did, but it's different now. Different when you see it."

"Yeah. Let's get out of here." I pulled Tania from the room. The cold was creeping up my arm until my forearm tingled with it. We stepped into the big room in time to meet Bruce, Mom, and Maggie, with a couple of the museum staff.

"There you are!" Mom said. "Well, we're all ready to move the sword."

This was maybe the toughest part of our plan. We had to keep Tania away from everybody, but especially Mom. "We'll just go down and wait for you by the front entrance," I said.

"Oh, we're not going that way. The museum has a van for us. We'll go out the back."

Lionel and I exchanged a glance. Between us, Tania looked down at her hand. She opened and closed it, as if it were a new experience. She looked up and opened her mouth, but I didn't know who would speak through it.

I said quickly, "Um, right, okay . . . a van, are you sure it's big enough? Maybe we should go ahead in a taxi, meet you there."

"You don't have to do that," Mom said. "If it's too crowded, we'll have Maggie and Lionel go in a taxi."

"You know what?" Lionel said. "These kids have never gone on the subway, have they?"

"Well, no," Mom said. "The taxis are usually faster, and almost as cheap if you have several people going a short distance."

"Sure, but really, you can't spend a week in New York and not ride the subway once!" Lionel grinned. "I'll tell you what, I'll take the kids on the subway. It will take you a while to load up, so we'll probably get there about the same time. And they'll have an important New York experience."

"Well, I guess that could work." Mom smiled at me and Tania. "Does that sound fun?"

"Sure, great," I said. Anything to get us out of there.

Lionel whispered something to Tania. She nodded. *"Oui."*

Maggie smiled. "Practicing your French again? Maybe you could talk to the ghost for us."

I laughed, a little too loud. Lionel gave a crazy grin and said, "Righto, we're off now. See you there."

We hurried from the room. As we crossed the museum, I said, "Are we really taking the subway? Won't it be full of people?"

"Hey, this is New York. They're used to crazy stuff on the subway. Trust me, they won't even blink."

"But it'll take time. Let's just get there as fast as possible."

"All right, there's a taxi." We hurried down the steps to where a taxi was already waiting in the street. Lionel ran ahead and opened the back door. Tania balked, almost pulling out of my grip and muttering something in French.

Lionel's eyebrows shot up. He said something back. A group of people went past, eyeing us curiously.

"What is it?" I asked. "Come on, let's go." I tried to push Tania into the taxi. She squirmed and babbled.

The taxi driver yelled, "You getting in?"

A man came up beside us. "Is this taxi free?"

Lionel said, "All yours." He closed the door behind the guy.

"What's going on?" I asked.

"She doesn't want to get in the taxi. I mean, he doesn't—the ghost. I guess it's not like anything he knew in his life."

People were starting to look at us. Lionel glanced around. "We can't walk all the way to The Monastery. Wait—there's the answer."

A horse and buggy clattered along the street. We'd seen a few in Central Park. It was funny to see carriages right in the city, but I guess it was a New York thing.

Lionel waved his arms and the man pulled over. "Care for a ride?"

"Can you take us up to The Monastery?"

He shook his head. "Too far. But I can take you through the park, a nice ride."

"All right, fine. Take us to the north end of the park, to a subway station." Lionel turned to me. "Get in." He added something in French to Tania.

We climbed up into the carriage. The driver flicked the reins and turned onto a road in the park.

Lionel spent the whole ride whispering to Tania in French. I didn't know what he was saying, and hoped the carriage driver didn't either. Since we couldn't really make plans in English with a stranger right there, I had to keep quiet.

I looked around, trying to enjoy the ride, but it wasn't easy. Too many questions bubbled in my brain. What had we gotten ourselves into? Was there any way this could possibly work? What if we couldn't get Tania and the ghost up to The Monastery? How would we get the ghost out of her?

The horse's hooves clattered. The smell of horse and manure drifted back over us. Cold radiated from Tania, a chill the sun couldn't warm. I looked out at the sun sparkling on a lake, wondering if I would have enjoyed this more on an average day.

I sighed. Nothing had been average for a long time. At least with Tania's gift, things stayed interesting, if not always safe.

It took ten or fifteen minutes to get through the park to a subway station. Lionel paid the driver while Tania and I got out. "What now?" I murmured. "The subway has to be at least as bad as a taxi, right?"

"I think I've explained it to him," Lionel said. "Anyway, once we're on and moving, he's pretty much stuck. A taxi driver would notice if we're wrestling with a girl who's trying to get out."

We hurried down the stairs into the station. Lionel bought a subway pass and grabbed a map as Tania looked around with her mouth open. We pushed through the turnstile to a long platform that smelled kind of stale. You could look down at the tracks and see the long metal rails, with damp, dark ground underneath. Lionel pulled us to the far end of the platform, which was deserted except for one old man slumped on a bench.

I took Tania's arm. It didn't seem as cold. Or was I just getting used to it? And if she wasn't as cold, what did that mean?

"Tania," I said. Her face turned to me, but her eyes looked strange. "Tania, are you still in there? Can you hear me? I want to talk to Tania."

Her words came out in French. I gripped her arm tighter. "I want to talk to my sister! Tania, you're in there somewhere."

Her eyes kind of clouded, changed a little. Her mouth opened and closed. "Jon?" It came out reedy thin.

Relief flooded me. "Tania! Don't let him take over completely. Keep some control. We're getting on the subway. It's going to be all right."

"All right." Was she just repeating my words, or did she understand?

A rumble started in the distance and grew louder, too loud for us to talk. The subway train roared toward us. It seemed to push cold air ahead of it. Lionel took Tania's other arm, and we held on tight, afraid she might freak out and run. It was pretty wild, all that noise and the huge metal train barreling down on us.

Tania pulled her arm out of my grasp and threw her hands up in front of her face. She screamed.

CHAPTER
25

Cold blasted through the station.

I stumbled back and hit the wall. Wind swirled around us, picking up scraps of newspaper and candy wrappers. My ears rang from the noise.

The train screeched to a stop, but Tania's wailing went on. Lionel threw his arms around her, holding her still and whispering in her ear.

The doors opened. A man and woman got off. The man said, "Feels like an early winter this year." His companion nodded and buttoned up her coat. The old man on the platform gave us a friendly smile and shuffled onto the train.

My pounding heart started to slow. Lionel took a deep breath and blew it out. He grinned at me. "Oh yeah, I love New York."

We dragged Tania into a subway car. She pulled

against us, babbling something, but she only weighs about seventy pounds, so even with the ghost in her we got her inside and seated. She stared around with wide eyes as the doors slid shut. The train rumbled, and the platform seemed to slide by.

Tania exclaimed, in a shrill voice. Lionel whispered to her. I looked around at the other passengers. Fortunately, there were only eight other people in the car. Some of them looked at us, but then went back to their book or magazine or dozing. My shoulders relaxed a little. I guess Lionel was right. It was kind of nice to be in a city where you could be as weird as you wanted, and no one cared.

For some reason that made me think of Mick. Would he have had friends if he had grown up in New York City? Would I have been different if I'd been born somewhere else?

I shook my head. I had enough to deal with in this life without playing "what if?"

Every time we pulled into a station, I tensed up. But whatever Lionel was saying to the ghost seemed to keep him calm. The rumble of the subway became soothing. I looked at the advertisements and subway maps. A few people got off. Only one new person got on. I wasn't sure how much time passed—in a way, it seemed endless.

"All right, this is us," Lionel said, as the train slowed again. We got out into the station. "Well, we have one piece of good news, anyway."

"What's that?" I asked.

"It won't be hard to convince the ghost to move on, once he does his duty by the sword. All this modern technology is just too much for him."

"Good," I said. "I'm about ready to have my sister back." It sounded strange as I said it, but it was true. Tania drove me crazy sometimes, but I only got this sick feeling in my stomach when she was sharing her body with a ghost.

We stepped out onto the street and looked around. "So where is this museum?" I asked.

Lionel studied his map. "It looks like we have to walk through that park. No taxis around, so let's go."

It would've been a great walk most days. The path wound through the park, and in places you could look out across a wide river, to the shore beyond. One sign described how this was the site of a battle in 1776. We passed bridges and statues and stone steps, fun places to explore if you had time. But I just wanted to get to The Monastery and be done with it all.

A man jogged by us, and a couple walking a dog gave us a smile. We passed a big rock outcropping, and then walked along the edge of a cliff. The wind picked up, blowing cold. I thought of how cold Tania already was. Could she get hypothermia from all this, or frostbite? I walked faster.

Finally, I saw a building ahead, light brown stone with a red tile roof. Lionel said, "There it is," and I heard the relief in his voice.

The windows were all arched, so it looked old and European. It was boxy, and low, except for one tower rising above the rest. It didn't look like a castle, but I remembered that it was supposed to be a monastery, where monks lived. That fit.

We followed the path around the side of the building and up a hill. The closer we got, the more we hurried. We passed through a small archway with a black iron gate, trotted up some stairs, and went through heavy wooden doors.

Tania murmured something.

"What?" I asked.

"He says it's beautiful here," Lionel said. "Like home."

My stomach did a flip. "He'd better not like it too much. He can't stay here. Not in Tania, anyway."

Lionel frowned, then shook his head. "Don't worry, they'd never let Tania stay here. If Hector Dubar wants to stick around after all, he'll have to do it as a ghost."

I knew he was right, but still. I imagined Tania speaking in French, fighting to stay in this museum, while we tried to drag her out. It wouldn't be pretty.

CHAPTER
26

We went through some doors and saw a counter with a woman behind it. "We're with the TV show," Lionel said. "Are they here yet?"

She smiled. "They arrived a few minutes ago. They're in the Benedictine Cloister." She spread out a map and pointed to it.

Tania started walking away, so I scurried after her. She was looking all around, at the old stone walls with medieval art. The room ahead looked like a small chapel. Tania headed for it, but I grabbed her arm. She turned and said something in French.

"Non," I said. I wanted to tell her we needed to hurry, but I had to settle for that.

Lionel caught up to us. "The Benedictine Cloister is on the lower level. They're probably still setting up."

"What do we do about Tania? She's acting too weird." She was gesturing at a statue and spouting something in

French. It was getting harder to see my sister inside. That was creepy. We couldn't wait too long to get rid of the ghost, or who knew what it might do to Tania. But we couldn't let Mom get near her either—or who knew what it might do to Mom.

"We need the sword and we need Marc, in order to do this transfer," Lionel said. "But I need to do his makeup first."

"We can't let the ghost see him without it."

Lionel took a deep breath. "All right, I'll go down first. Keep Tania and Hector out of the way. Give me twenty minutes."

I looked at Tania, who was reaching out for a statue. I grabbed her arm as a guard took a step toward us. We turned and pulled Tania down a corridor. "Then what?" I whispered. "How do we get the sword?"

Lionel shrugged. "I guess we wing it."

He jogged off, and I let Tania lead the way through the museum. We went along corridors with stone arches and carved columns along the sides. Down some stairs we found a little room called the Gothic Chapel. It had stone caskets with carved figures lying on the top, stuff that might have been interesting if I hadn't been so worried.

I kept looking at my watch. Within fifteen minutes, I was waiting by the Benedictine Cloister. It was a court-yard with flowers and brick paths, with a small stone fountain in the center. A brick walkway went all the way around the courtyard, separated from it by a low stone wall. Columns joined that low wall to the walkway roof. You could stand on the walkway and look between the columns into the courtyard. I saw Mom, Bruce, and Maggie with the camera operators and a couple of other people.

I pushed Tania back into a corner of the corridor. "Stay. Wait." I searched my mind for any hint of how to say those things in French, but came up blank. I just hoped she understood.

I slipped into the courtyard. Finally I spotted Lionel, in the corridor on the other side. He was adjusting Marc's jacket. When he saw me he snapped his makeup case shut and gave a nod.

Mom looked up and said, "There you are! We were starting to think you got lost."

I smiled. "Nope, just looking around."

Maggie asked, "Did you see the tapestries? They're my favorites." She glanced around. "I figured Tania would like them."

"Um, we must have missed them. Tania's still looking at something back there." I gestured vaguely back the way I had come.

"We'll start filming in a few minutes," Mom said. "Just as soon as everyone's ready."

I spotted the sword, lying on a piece of cloth on one of the low walls around the courtyard. Two guys from the museum stood on either side, like guards.

"Um, maybe Marc should practice with the sword," I said. "You know, we could take it into another room, and he could get used to the weight."

"Good idea!" Lionel hurried over. "I still have to work on the fellow who's playing the part of the squire. Maybe Jon and Tania could practice handing off the sword to Marc."

"Don't bother," Mom said. "We'll just have the actors run through it a couple of times before we start the cameras."

One of the museum guys took a step toward us. "The sword should stay right here until we're ready to film. We don't want it handled any more than necessary."

Lionel and I looked at each other. He gave a little shrug.

Whatever we did, we'd have to do it right there in front of everyone.

Lionel and I moved to the side and spoke in low voices. "Oh, man," Lionel said. "How are we going to do this?"

"We have to just go for it," I said. "We can't leave the squire in Tania much longer."

"All right, okay. What do you want me to do?"

I tried to get my brain around all the things that had to happen for this to work. "Marc is in costume and makeup, but we have to make sure he says the right thing. If Tania comes up to him, he has to talk to her in French."

"All right, leave Marc to me."

"But you need to talk to Hector Dubar as well, since I can't. If we're lucky, he'll be willing to just walk up to Marc and say something, and leave the sword sitting there." And if we weren't lucky? I didn't want to think about that.

Lionel nodded. "You go get Tania. I'll get Marc set up, tell him we need to practice and work out what he should say."

"Okay. Be ready."

I jogged around the walkway outside the courtyard. Mom, Bruce, and Maggie were busy setting up. I hoped they'd stay busy for a while.

I got back to the corner where I'd left Tania. I groaned out loud. Of course she was gone.

CHAPTER
27

I ran to the nearest doorway and looked around. I saw a family with little kids, and an older couple talking in some foreign language. No Tania.

I turned right and ran down the hallway, guessing randomly, hoping. A guard shouted at me. "Hey, no running!" I slowed to a very fast walk.

I turned into a room with lots of glass cases, went out the other end, and in a circle back to where I'd started. The guard eyed me again. I didn't want to walk down that long room with him watching me, so I turned up some stairs.

They led to a small room with just a couple of tourists. I kept moving. I had no idea where I was. How big was this place?

I squeezed past a guy almost blocking a doorway. This room was crowded and had rugs or something hanging on the walls.

"Tania!" I gasped. My second of relief quickly faded. A big guard in uniform had Tania by the arms. She was struggling and calling him a *cochon Anglais*.

"Look, missy," the guard said. "I told you not to touch. I think it's time you got out of here."

I ran up to them. "Hi! Sorry. I'll take her out."

He frowned at me. "She's with you?"

"Yeah, sorry she's, uh . . . a foreign exchange student! Doesn't speak English. Doesn't know the rules. I'm sure it was all just an accident."

"Uh-huh. She was opening the drawers in that cabinet."

"They do that in her country, touch things in museums," I said, smiling widely at the guard.

"Well don't let her do it here. She shouldn't be wandering around on her own, if she doesn't know better."

"No, no. I just turned my back for second and she got away from me." I tried to pry Tania's arm out of his hand.

"Make sure it doesn't happen again. You here with your parents?" He still had a hold of Tania's other arm.

"Yes, they're just around the corner. We'll go right to them. It's okay." I pulled on Tania, and he let her go, though he kept glaring.

"See she doesn't get into any more trouble."

"I will! She won't!" I dragged Tania from the room.

She was still shouting French insults over her shoulder. At least the guard didn't seem to understand French. One of the tourists was laughing, though.

I let Tania babble as I dragged her through the museum. I was glad she was my *little* sister. What would we do if we had a ghost invading some two-hundred-pound guy?

I couldn't remember which way I'd come, so first I just worried about getting away from the guard. I saw an open courtyard and headed for it. When I got there, I realized it was the wrong one. I groaned. How long was this going to take?

I took a deep breath and tried to think, ignoring Tania's rambling but keeping a grip on her arm. Wait, I'd come up some stairs. Somehow we needed to get back down.

I went through a doorway in a direction that felt vaguely right. A woman guard stood in the corner of the room. My first instinct was to turn back and run, but I told myself she wouldn't know what Tania had been up to.

"Shhh," I hissed to Tania. I smiled at the guard. "Can you tell us how to get down to the lower level?"

She gestured toward an opening farther along in the room. "Right down there."

I kept my grin in place and pretended I wasn't hurrying as we crossed the room. The stairs led down to the long room I recognized, and soon we were back out by the courtyard.

I was sweaty and trembling, my heart still hammering. I felt like I'd been playing sports, not visiting a museum. But the TV crew was still busy setting up, and I realized I'd probably only been gone ten minutes. It was a funny thing about being around ghosts—they make you feel like you're living through lifetimes.

Tania said something in French. "Stop it," I said, shaking her arm. I turned her, held her shoulders, and looked into her eyes. "Tania, pay attention. Stop letting the ghost take over. We're going to need your help."

Big blue eyes looked back at me, familiar yet somehow different. I got a cold ache in my stomach. That's when I realized that Tania's skin no longer felt cold. No icy waves rolled off of her. She looked and felt like a normal eleven-year-old girl.

But not quite like my sister.

I shook her. "Tania! Don't do this to me! You have to be in there too. Fight back, do something!"

She smiled. And her voice said something in French.

I grabbed her arm and pulled her along the walkway. "We have to get this over with. Now!"

CHAPTER
28

I looked through one of the open arches into the courtyard. Maggie was laughing. Bruce fiddled with his hair. Mom gave instructions to Stephan, the cameraman. I realized Mick wasn't there. Maybe he'd stayed home with his headache. Good—we didn't need anything to trigger his memory now.

I took a deep breath and tried to pretend my heart wasn't pounding. I took Tania's arm. "Chev-al-ee-yay," I said, hoping I was pronouncing it more or less right. That was the word they'd been using for knight.

Tania came with me, babbling excitedly. I tried to shush her and hoped no one inside the courtyard would notice us as we passed by.

The scene in the courtyard kept appearing and disappearing as we passed columns and archways, column, arch, column, arch.

Maggie glanced up and smiled. "Almost ready," she called.

Sweat dripped along my cheek. For once, I wished they'd take longer to set up.

Bruce said, "Lionel, come on, I need my makeup."

We rounded the corner. Lionel was putting makeup on the other actor, a guy I'd hardly noticed. He was tall and handsome, with blond hair. I thought how different he looked from how Tania had described the ghost—let alone how the ghost looked now, in Tania's body.

"All right, you're fine," Lionel said to the actor. "Just go out there and wait."

The actor swaggered into the courtyard as I dragged Tania up to Lionel. He nodded. "Marc knows what to do." Lionel whispered something to Tania, then he turned and clapped his hands. "All right, Marc, let's do a quick run-through. I want to make sure your makeup looks all right while moving."

"Sure, whatever you say." Marc looked good in the old-fashioned costume, with a black jacket over a white shirt, and black leather boots that came all the way up his thighs. Much more impressive than in jeans and a T-shirt, though you'd never catch me in a getup like that. "Shall I call Roy back?" he asked.

"Oh no," Lionel said. "No need. Tania's been practicing her French. She can run through it with you."

Lionel switched to French, said something, then nodded to Marc. Marc stepped forward and made a big bow, with a sweep of his hand. It looked kind of silly to me, but maybe that's really how they did it back then. He straightened, smiling.

Tania moved toward him, hands clasped together reverently. Her face shone as she trilled something in French.

Marc's eyebrows went up. "Hey, that's pretty good!"

"Remember your lines," Lionel said.

"But that stuff, about serving my ancestor—that's not in the script. I'm supposed to be the actual knight, right?"

"Just go with it." Lionel grinned through his teeth. "Think of it as improv practice."

Tania was watching Marc, frowning. He had to stop speaking in English! I didn't realize I'd been holding my breath until it all came out in a *whoosh*. I felt like I was watching a performance, something I couldn't control, and sometimes couldn't even understand. But I was still responsible for it, like I was the director or something.

Marc spoke in French. I heard a word that sounded kind of like honor. It is an honor to meet you? Your honor is fulfilled? I could only guess.

Tania turned and moved toward the sword, which was lying on the low wall a few paces away. I leaped after her, without thinking, without knowing what I would do. I just wanted to be ready. At least the museum guys were on the other side of the wall, looking out into the courtyard at the TV crew.

Mom called out, "Come on, everyone, get into your places. Marc, are you ready? Lionel, please touch up Bruce's makeup, and then let's get this show on the road."

Tania reached for the sword. One of the museum guys turned his head.

Tania's hands slid under the sword. I opened my mouth, but I couldn't think of what to say. Stop? Hurry?

She lifted the sword. The museum guy said, "Hey!" He reached for her, but they had the low wall between them. "Put that down!" He started to climb over the wall. The other museum guy turned.

Tania held the sword horizontal, in both hands. She had a look of utter happiness on her face as she knelt in front of Marc. She held the sword up to him.

"Uh . . ." He glanced at the museum guys, and then at Lionel.

"Just take it," Lionel hissed.

Marc leaned down and lifted the sword from Tania's hands. "All right, well done. I mean—" He said something in French.

The first museum guy was over the wall and coming

toward them. The second wasn't far behind.

Tania looked up, tears wet in her eyes. She murmured something. Her eyes closed.

Lionel nudged my arm. "We did it!" he whispered.

I jumped forward and grabbed Tania's shoulders. I hauled her up and away from Marc.

The museum guys converged on us. "That is not a toy!" one of them said.

Lionel pushed in front of Tania and me. "All right, we were just practicing. No harm done."

Marc handed the sword back. Tania hung limp in my arms. The people in the courtyard were walking closer. I tried to pull Tania out of sight behind a column.

"What on earth is going on?" Mom asked. "Come on, we don't have all day."

Bruce whined, "What about my makeup?"

I dragged Tania to the nearest doorway. I hoped the ghost was gone. I hoped my sister was back. But I didn't know how long it would take her to recover—if she did. I just needed to get away from all those people. Then hope and pray I could deal with whatever happened next.

CHAPTER
29

We stumbled into another courtyard. I leaned Tania against a wall and glanced around to make sure we were alone.

Tania's eyes rolled back in her head. She started sliding through my grasp. "Tania!" I lowered her to the ground. Her legs folded, and she wound up in a heap, leaning against me.

"Come on, Tania, wake up. Don't do this to me." Should I shake her? Yell for help? Call an ambulance?

I tipped her head back, tried to see if she was breathing, fumbled at her throat for a pulse. My own heart was pounding so loudly, I couldn't hear anything else.

My vision blurred, and an image rose up before me. My baby sister, Angela, lying in a hospital bed. Eaten away by cancer. The life draining out of her so quickly you could see it.

I patted Tania's face. "Come on, wake up. We need you. Mom needs you. I need you."

She moaned. Her eyelids fluttered.

I might have sobbed. "Tania!"

"Umph, you're hurting me," she mumbled.

I loosened my grip. "Don't you ever, ever, *ever* scare me like that again!"

Tania pulled up her knees and rested her head on them. I leaned against the wall, letting my heart slow, feeling the sweat cold on my face.

A bit of movement caught my eye. I watched Maggie walk toward us. I couldn't even make myself move.

"Are you two okay?"

I looked at Tania. She nodded and mumbled, "I'm all right." But she didn't look all right.

"She just felt a little faint," I told Maggie. "But she's okay now." I tried to grin. "She just forgot to eat again."

Maggie frowned. She reached into her bag, pulled out a granola bar and solemnly handed it to Tania. Tania fumbled with the wrapper.

"There's no need to tell Mom." I tried to sound casual. "You know how she worries. But it's nothing."

Maggie shook her head. "Sometimes I don't know what to do with you kids."

I gazed up at her, begging her to trust me. "Look,

you know when we first met, at the haunted hotel? You said if we ever needed to talk about something, we could talk to you and you wouldn't tell Mom or Bruce."

She nodded and gave a crooked smile. "Does that mean you're actually going to talk to me?"

I wanted to. I really did. It was hard keeping all this a secret. Maggie was a friend, and she was smart, and could help. But it wasn't just my secret. It was Tania's first. She nibbled the granola bar, hardly aware of us. She couldn't make a decision now.

And I remembered what I'd said about Mick. The fewer people who knew, the better. Lionel knew now, and Mick might remember. How many people could we tell, and still call it a secret?

I swallowed hard. "Maybe. Not just yet, but . . . maybe soon."

She sighed, and looked sad. "I really wish you could trust me."

"We do trust you! It's just—" I shrugged. "Sometimes it's not just about trust."

She gave me a long look. "All right, I guess I can understand that. Well, when you're ready, I'll be here."

She turned and walked away. I felt like I'd lost something. At least we had Lionel. He wasn't Maggie, but it helped to have one grown-up who knew, who would be there next time.

I could hear voices from the Benedictine Cloister. I glanced down at Tania, who had her head against her knees. I'd just seen the real exchange—what did I care about the reenactment?

I thought about the squire, staying behind so many years to fulfill his duty. It seemed sort of stupid, protecting the sword for a knight who didn't need it anymore, and must have gone on—wherever people went—years ago. But admirable, too. Honorable. He kept trying to do his duty, even after death.

I glanced down at Tania again. Was this my duty—my destiny?—to carry her sword while she went on her crusade? And was that pathetic, or something to be proud of?

I thought of Mom and Maggie working behind the scenes while Bruce got all the glory as the TV show host. Was that fair? Did they mind? Would it all be different someday?

I sighed, leaned back, and closed my eyes. Maybe someday Tania would stop seeing ghosts. Maybe I'd have to find my own quest. But for now, this was my life.

CHAPTER
30

We had a kind of celebration in the hotel lounge, on our last night in New York City. Bruce thought he had enough material for a good show. "We'll make people forget about Madame Natasha," he said. "We have to. We'll make this show a success."

I hoped he was right. Tania and I still owed him a favor.

Tania and I sat in a corner, taking it easy, while the crew laughed and chatted. Lionel plopped down beside us. "Well, I want to thank you kids for an interesting experience."

"Hey, this is just the beginning," I said. I'd meant it as a joke, but as I said it I knew it was true. We had lots of adventures ahead, and they wouldn't always be fun or easy—but they would be interesting.

He nodded, and looked serious for a second, then

broke into a grin. "It's a whole new beginning for me. The best chance of my life!"

I thought he meant learning about ghosts, helping us, something like that. But he went on. "I'm staying in New York. Marc helped me get a job at the theater. I've been putting it off too long, taking this risk."

I stared at him. He was abandoning us now, just when I'd thought we had help? Heat rose up inside me, and a sick feeling.

But Lionel looked so happy. "I'm thirty-five, and it's time I stopped visiting New York and promising myself I'll move here someday." He started singing. "'If I can make it here, I'll make it anywhere . . . '"

My anger faded. Maybe this was his quest. "Good luck," I said.

"Thanks—you too!" He patted my shoulder, winked at Tania, and went to join Marc.

A few minutes later, Maggie came over to us. "You kids are quiet tonight."

"It's been a long week," I said.

"Get used to it. That's how these shoots work."

I tried to think of something else to say. "So what's the next one?"

She frowned. "It's kind of a crazy idea Bruce had. I hope he can pull it off."

"What do you mean?"

"There's a story about a German miner, back in the 1870s. Supposedly he found this amazing gold mine. He showed up in town with gold nuggets and fantastic stories. Problem was, he could never find the mine again. He wandered the mountains for years, until he died. Other people have tried to find the mine, and failed. But some people have said they've seen the German miner's ghost."

"He's still out there?" Tania asked. It was the first she'd spoken in a while. "Still looking for the mine?"

"That the idea," Maggie said. "Bruce wants to find the ghost. But it won't be easy. I mean, even if there is such a ghost, he's supposed to be wandering."

"Still, it sound like a cool trip," I said.

"Oh, it should be." Maggie grinned. "We're going in on horseback and mule, taking our camping gear for a few days. Quite the adventure."

"Awesome!" I said.

"I sure hope so. It will be interesting, living together like that. We may get to know each other better than we ever wanted to." She grimaced. "At least we won't have to deal with Madame Natasha."

I kind of winced, but I nodded. I couldn't be sorry we'd gotten rid of her, even if I was sorry about what it did to the show's reputation.

"Well, take it easy," Maggie said. She wandered off.

"Should be a cool next episode," I said to Tania.

She was bouncy again, the color back in her face. "It's perfect! This is our chance!"

"What do you mean?" I almost hated to ask.

Tania's eyes shone. "To help Bruce and the show! To make up for humiliating him with Madame Natasha."

"You mean we help them find this ghost?"

She nodded. "But we have to make sure the show gets some good footage, before we help the ghost move on."

"Okay . . . " I had no idea how we'd do that. I guess we were learning to improvise, too. "But no letting him take you over. That's getting too dangerous."

Tania's fingers drummed the arm of her chair as she watched Bruce and Mom across the room. "And you know what would be great?"

I cringed. "What?"

"If we could actually find the ghost miner's treasure!"

I stared at her for a second. Then I started laughing. "Sure, why not? Otherwise it wouldn't be enough of a challenge."

CHECK OUT SOME OTHER GHOSTLY BOOKS FROM ALADDIN:

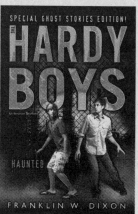

From Aladdin
Published by Simon & Schuster

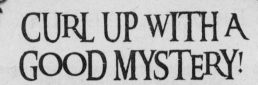